TRAITORS
AMONG
US

Also by Marsha Forchuk Skrypuch

TRAITORS AMONG US

A novel by
MARSHA FORCHUK SKRYPUCH

SCHOLASTIC PRESS / NEW YORK

Library of Congress Cataloging-in-Publication Data available

ISBN 978-1-338-75430-8

10 9 8 7 6 5 4 3 2 1   21 22 23 24 25

Printed in the U.S.A.   113

First printing, September 2021

Book design by Yaffa Jaskoll

TO MY SISTERS, CHERYL, GEORGIA,
AND LARA—WITH LOVE.

CHAPTER ONE–
WE ARE SAFE
KRYSTIA

Refugee Camp, American Zone, Karlsfeld, Germany, June 1945

I pulled myself up to the top bunk, then reached down and grasped my younger sister's hand, steadying her as she climbed in beside me.

"I'm so tired," said Maria, leaning her head on my shoulder.

"Let's lie down, then," I said.

Maria put her lips to my ear. "We should see who else comes into our barrack first."

Exhaustion weighed me down like a heavy blanket, and I felt as if I could sleep for an eternity, but Maria was right. We had to see who else ended up in this barrack with us.

1

A familiar woman with a worry-lined face stepped through the entrance.

"Hello, Dasha," said Maria. "The cot beneath us is still free."

When she was on the road with us, Dasha had had a dead infant tied to her back, but now it was gone. Did the Americans take the infant when she entered the camp? Or maybe she had given it up willingly, now that she was on protected territory.

Dasha shuffled toward us. "It's good to see familiar faces," she said. Then she slumped into the lowest of the two bunks below us with a sigh.

More people came in. Some of them I recognized from our long trek, including a mother with a toddler. She took the bunk between us and Dasha. When a sturdy girl with blond braids stepped in, Maria gasped. The girl seemed to have too much fat on her bones to be a refugee. Besides that, her hair and clothing looked suspiciously clean. I reached up and patted down my own hair, removing a bit of leaf and a twig as I did so. Who stayed clean and fresh while sleeping in bushes and muddy gutters? Not a real refugee, that was for sure.

The girl surveyed the room and her gaze fell on my sister. Her eyes narrowed. Maria's fingernails dug into my palm. The girl took a top bunk on the opposite side of the barrack—right across from us. Once she was settled in, she turned her back to us and appeared to sleep.

"Do you know that girl, Maria?" I whispered.

"That's Sophie Huber. Frau Huber's daughter."

Frau Huber was the owner of the farm where Maria had been a forced laborer.

"So she's not a refugee," I said.

"She certainly isn't," said Maria. "She's a Hitler Girl, a member of the League of German Girls. She tormented non-Aryans like me. I bet she doesn't want to go home. She'd be caught and punished."

"We should report her to the Americans," I said.

Maria nodded, her eyes trained on Sophie's back. "Should we go right now?"

"First thing tomorrow morning," I said. Then I stretched out on the straw-filled mattress, smoothing down my trousers, blouse, and jacket, wishing they were as presentable as the Hitler Girl's clothing.

Maria stayed sitting up, with her eyes glued to Sophie's back.

"You're tired," I whispered, tugging on her jacket. "Sleep now."

Finally she sighed and flopped down beside me. "My feet are aching," she said. "I'd love to take off my shoes."

"You can't," I said. "Someone could steal them, and then you'd be barefoot like me."

"Do your feet hurt too?" she asked.

Her question made my toes wiggle in response. My ankles ached and so did the joints in both big toes, but the soles of my feet were protected by thick, leathery calluses from all our walking. About a week ago, I had stepped on a piece of shrapnel, but that cut had miraculously not gotten infected, and it was mostly healed. But I did not want my fourteen-year-old sister walking around in bare feet. She could easily step on something sharp, and because her feet weren't toughened up like mine, that could be a disaster. I was the older sister, and it was my responsibility to keep her safe.

"Believe me," I told Maria. "You don't want to lose your shoes."

Maria grunted, then cuddled in beside me. I closed my eyes and tried to sleep. But the thought of a Hitler Girl posing as a refugee sleeping across from us was distracting, to say the least. I tried to erase the anger by concentrating on the good:

Maria and I both had full stomachs.

The war was over.

Maria and I were safe.

Maria and I were together, just like Mama wanted.

The Americans were protecting us.

Soon we'd be able to go to Canada!

Auntie Stefa, in Toronto, would look after us as if we were her own daughters. The Red Cross lady had given us paper and a pencil to write a letter to Auntie Stefa when we first got here. She'd even taken our photograph and said she'd add it to an envelope with our letter once the picture was developed and printed. Once Auntie got our letter and photograph, I knew she'd come and get us!

My eyes felt gritty from the white powder the nurse had sprayed on us to kill the lice that all the refugees carried. I drifted in and out of sleep and dreamed I was back on the road with thousands of refugees fleeing the fighting, first in Ukraine, then in Austria. But the war zone kept catching up with us.

All of a sudden, there was a scraping sound at the door. Or was it just a part of my dreams? I sat up and looked around. I wasn't on that road anymore, and there was no fighting, just exhausted, ragged people, all trying their best to settle into sleep. I reached up to the ceiling and put a fingertip through one of the many bullet holes that had pierced the barrack. Bits of dimming daylight shone through the holes, making odd shapes and shadows throughout our shelter. The only sounds were the weeping, snores, and chatter of my fellow refugees.

I looked down at my sister beside me, expecting to see her fast asleep, but her eyes were wide open and her jaw was clenched. I caressed her cheek with a featherlight touch. "Sleep, Maria. We're together. We're safe. We'll be in Canada soon."

She closed her eyes, but I stayed propped up on my arm so I could watch as she slowly drifted off. Only when she was sound asleep did I lie back down and close my own eyes.

Why had I assured Maria that we were safe when I had no way of knowing if that was true?

CHAPTER TWO–
THE RUSSIAN CHILD
MARIA

Once I heard Krystia's breathing settle into the rhythm of sleep, I opened my eyes and sat up, propping my back against the frame of our bunk. I loved my sister, and it was sweet that she thought she needed to look after me, but she was just sixteen, and she was not my mother! I looked after her as much as she looked after me, whether she acknowledged it or not. She was exhausted and she needed her sleep, but someone needed to keep a lookout.

Sophie hadn't turned around even once since she'd crawled into that bunk across from us, but she didn't fool me. She was no more asleep than I was. How had she tricked her way into a refugee camp in the first place? And of all the barracks in all the refugee camps in the entire

Allied zone, why did that horrible girl have to be assigned to ours?

In the dimness, a man in the bunk just beneath Sophie's got up and stretched. She bolted upright, but the man whispered in a kind voice, "Go back to sleep, child. I just needed to move around a bit."

Moments later, there was the crunch of tires on gravel nearby and the low growl of a truck motor. Bootsteps sounded outside our door.

In my hazy state, I first thought it was just a dream, but we had to stay alert. While we were on the road, even after the Nazis were defeated and were no longer a threat, we were still in constant danger of violence, but from the Soviets now. Red Army soldiers would go into houses and stores and steal whatever they could carry. Shattered bottles, spoiled food, and ripped clothing were scattered in their wake. But the worst thing was that they attacked girls and women, whether they were German or refugee, child or grandmother. It didn't seem to matter to them, as long as they were female. I could have devoured the food that those Soviets left half-eaten, but it wasn't safe to come out of hiding.

I heard another crunch of gravel. Someone was right outside our door.

"Krystia," I whispered, shaking her shoulder. "Wake up."

She jerked up and rubbed her eyes.

I pointed to the door. "Someone just pulled up in a truck."

She inhaled sharply. "We need to hide."

"Where?"

"The crawl space under the bottom bunk," she said.

I slid off our bunk and flattened myself onto the floor as quietly as I could, but Sophie heard. And in the dim light, I saw her turn. I met her startled gaze for one second, then squirmed into the crawl space beneath the lowest bunk. From my vantage point I saw Krystia's feet hit the ground, and then she stretched herself onto the floor, but when she tried to wriggle in beside me, her pants caught on a sliver of wood. I grabbed the waist of her trousers and pulled hard. The sliver snapped, and she was free. She squeezed in beside me. I couldn't see a thing because she blocked my view, but there was a crash of boots against the door and a screech as it opened.

"You," shouted a man's voice in Russian. "Show me your papers. You. Stand by the door."

The soldier's footsteps were loud as he went down the aisle, stopping at each set of bunks and examining papers. It relieved me a little bit that he was acting official and was therefore less likely to come in here just to hurt girls. It was hard to make out why some refugees were ordered to line up at the door and others were left where they were. Most of the people from our barrack were the refugees who had been with us on the road. They had fled the farms and factories where they had been forced to work for the Nazis when their countries had been conquered. They were from all over Europe and were all different ages. I'm sure that many of them, like my sister and me, had no home to return to and were just trying to stay alive until they could find some place to live.

There were rumors that the Soviets would be trying to capture anyone who had ever been a Soviet citizen and take them to the Soviet Union, whether they wanted to go or not. I had no way of knowing if the rumor was true. Maybe the Soviets were just looking for criminals. There were well-fed people hiding among the refugees. Those who had profited from Hitler's rule. Like Sophie. Maybe that was the kind of person this soldier was looking for.

I heard a shuffle, rustling of paper, and a slap. "Stand by the door," said the soldier.

I heard the boots stop in front of our bunk, and I held my breath.

"Off the bunk and give me your papers," the soldier demanded.

Above us, the bottom bunk squeaked and there was a shuffle of bare feet on the ground as Dasha obeyed. Paper rustled again.

Dasha's bunk squeaked above us as she climbed back in, stirring up dust that tickled my nose. I could feel a sneeze coming on but held it in. Dasha was not selected. Her hometown was close to ours in Ukraine and had been invaded by the Soviet Union in 1939, just like ours had. Then when the Nazis invaded in 1941, she had ended up as a slave laborer for them, just like I had.

Maybe Krystia and I would have been safe even if we hadn't hidden. Relief washed over me. This would all be over soon.

"Show me your papers," the soldier said, still standing in front of our bunk. He must have been speaking to the woman with the toddler.

The woman said in a shaky voice, "We're British."

"How did you end up here?" he asked.

"We're being transferred to the British zone tomorrow," she said.

"But how did you end up in the war zone in Germany, a British mother and young child?" asked the soldier.

"I, it's, um . . . a long story," she replied.

There was more rustling of papers, then the soldier said, "Olga Krasnov. The boy is Piotr Krasnov. These are British papers, but your names sound Russian."

"But I was born in Britain, and so was my son."

"You're a Russian traitor, aren't you?" said the soldier

in an angry voice. "Shame on you, fighting against the Soviets. Come with me."

"I can assure you that I did not fight," said Olga in old-fashioned Russian. "And besides, we're British . . ."

There was a slap, then a thump and a toddler's scream. "Do what I say if you want your child back," said the soldier.

The toddler stopped crying, and I could only hope that meant the soldier had given him back to the mother, but how could the Soviets possibly justify taking a mother and son with papers identifying them as British citizens? It was hard to figure out who was safe and who wasn't.

The boots clomped to a different bunk. I slowly let out my breath. He hadn't noticed us. We were safe. But then I heard Sophie say, "Officer, there are two Nazi collaborators hiding under that bunk."

CHAPTER THREE- HOMECOMING
KRYSTIA

I watched in horror as the soldier's boots turned, then stepped back to our bunk. Next, his knees settled onto the ground and his face appeared just centimeters away from mine. He'd lost a front tooth, and his breath smelled of garlic. He was not smiling.

"Get out or I'll drag you out," he said in a surprisingly controlled voice.

I tried to slide out, but my clothes caught on the wood slivers again. And it didn't help that I was nearly paralyzed with fear. The soldier grabbed my arm and pulled. Hard.

I stumbled to my feet and shook the slivers of wood from my trousers. As I surveyed the room, I noticed a second soldier standing by the entrance with a rifle aimed at a cluster of refugees. There was the English woman and her toddler son, as well as a red-haired boy about my age and a man who looked too well-fed to be a refugee.

Maria slid out from under the bunk and stood beside me, shaking cobwebs from her face and hair.

"Both of you. Stand with that group," said the soldier.

"But our papers are in order," I said, pulling mine out of my pocket. I handed him my German passport, my work papers, plus the paper from the Americans identifying me as a refugee. "You shouldn't believe that girl. We are not Nazi collaborators."

"You were hiding, and that means you're guilty of something," said the soldier.

I grabbed Maria's hand. With our heads high, we walked to the group at the door. Did I regret hiding under the bunks? Not for a minute. Hiding from soldiers is what had kept me and Maria alive. I'd do it again without hesitation.

From her top bunk, Sophie watched us with a smirk, but it was quickly replaced by a look of panic, because the soldier followed my glare. He stepped in front of Sophie.

"Your accent," he said. "You're German."

Austrian, I felt like saying, but I kept my mouth shut. And by Sophie's expression, I think she wished that she had kept her mouth shut as well.

"Papers," he said.

She handed him a document. He unfolded it and looked up at her. "You're not from Warsaw."

"Yes, I am, Officer."

He shook the paper under her nose. "This is a stolen document."

Sophie went still. "No, Officer, my name is Bianka Holata. I've been a slave laborer at the Huber farm for so long that I guess I've picked up a bit of an accent."

"Go to the door," said the soldier.

"You don't have the right," said Sophie. "Warsaw was never part of the Soviet Union."

The soldier slapped Sophie's cheek with such force that she nearly fell off the bunk.

"You're not Bianka Holata, and you're not from Warsaw," said the soldier. "I bet you're a Werewolf."

A Werewolf? We had heard rumors of that movement, but did it really exist? Hitler Boys and Girls working underground, trying to bring the Nazis back to power? I looked over to Maria, who was blinking back tears. She knew all about Sophie, and about the real Bianka, her dear friend and fellow slave laborer at the Huber farm. We both knew what kind of person Sophie was, but we stayed silent. Others in our barrack muttered and whispered, but no one said out loud what we were probably all thinking.

The soldier wrenched Sophie's arm, pulling her down

from the bunk. "I'm not stupid. Over there, now. It won't take long to find out who you really are."

With a hand covering her slapped cheek, Sophie walked over to join our group.

The soldier at the entrance opened the door wide. "Out," he said in a raspy voice, shoving us with the butt of his rifle. As we stumbled out of the barrack, I saw a truck illuminated by moonlight, the back doors yawning open. The two soldiers pushed and prodded us toward it.

The man and boy got in without a fight. This was an American camp. Weren't we protected? When it was my turn, I crossed my arms and looked the garlic-breathed soldier in the eye. "I'm not going with you. Shoot me if you want."

The soldier roughly grabbed Maria by the waistband. "I'll do better than that," he said. "I'll kill your sister instead."

The raspy-voiced soldier snatched Piotr from Olga's arms and dangled him by the ankles. The child screamed.

"Two for the price of one," he said, chuckling. "Get in *now* or this kid *and* your sister will both get a bullet in the head."

"Don't shoot, please!" I screamed.

"I'll count to three," said the soldier holding Maria. "If everyone isn't up in the truck by then, these two will die. One . . ."

It was a big step into the truck from the ground,

and Olga was having trouble, distracted by her toddler's shrieks. I boosted her up by the bum, then scrambled in myself.

"Two . . . ," said the soldier.

Sophie hesitated. I felt like slapping her.

"Three . . . ," said the soldier just as Sophie slowly crawled in.

"You're lucky," he said as he released Maria's waistband.

Maria grabbed Piotr from the other soldier and passed him up to Olga, and then I helped her in. She slumped down beside me and hissed into my ear, "That was an incredibly stupid thing to do."

"Shh," I responded.

"Don't shush me every time I have something to say," she whispered.

I placed a finger on her lips to make her stop talking. I could hear the soldiers conversing in Russian, and I tried to make out the words but couldn't hear anything that was useful except that the one with the garlic breath was named Misha and the one with a raspy voice was Vlad. They laughed and seemed to be pleased about a job well done.

We slumped onto the floor as the truck began to move.

"The Americans will stop them at the gate," said the man who had been captured with us. "There's still time to get out of this mess."

The truck came to a stop, and the doors opened, letting in a whoosh of air. Misha and an American soldier stood side by side. The American flashed a light into each of our faces.

"So, these are all Soviet citizens?" he asked in rudimentary Russian.

"They are," said Misha.

"Officer, please help me!" cried Olga in English. "I'm British."

Misha shook his head and gave the American soldier a patient smile. "What a character." He shuffled through our documents and pulled one out. "You'll see here that her name is clearly Russian, but she's traveling on a forged passport."

The American hesitated for a moment. "Are you sure?"

"She's known to us," said Misha.

"Okay," said the American. Then he smiled at us all. "Have a good trip home."

"But we're being abducted . . . ," I shouted.

The doors slammed shut, and we were plunged back into darkness. The soldier may have spoken basic Russian, but he ignored my Ukrainian.

"Maybe it would have been better to be shot," said Maria.

I squeezed her hand. "Never," I said. "I'll keep you safe."

CHAPTER FOUR-
VOLKSDEUTSCHE
MARIA

The motor revved, and the truck lurched forward. I leaned my head on Krystia's shoulder and patted her forearm comfortingly. She had risked my life with her heroics but still thought that she was the one saving me.

It was too dark to see anything, but I could hear the other captives settling in around us. The boy and man sat beside me. Piotr let out a whimper across from us, and Olga sang a soft lullaby.

Sophie must have found a spot as far away from us as she could. Good thing too, because if she was near us, I probably would have punched her. What a thief she was, taking Bianka's papers like that.

And then for Sophie to call *us* Nazi collaborators when she might even be a Werewolf. Sophie, the Jugend, the

Hitler Girl, calling us collaborators. How dare she? Anger roiled in my stomach like a poison.

This whole situation was terrifying. Here I had thought we were finally safe. We'd survived the Nazis, after all.

But what did the Soviets want with us? Judging by the other people they took, it wasn't just a matter of taking back Soviet citizens. They seemed to think each of us had done something bad. How could we get out of this? I tried to think.

The truck rumbled along with a lulling motion that made my eyelids heavy. So much for thinking.

Against my will, I slept.

Mama. Her face shines like a pearl, and there are no wrinkles. Her hair is smoothed into a bun at the nape of her neck, and she wears her favorite sky-blue blouse, although now it seems unfrayed.

I reach out to touch her hand, but hers is made of vapor. My heart aches. "I'm sorry for leaving you, Mama."

She reaches her fingertips to my cheek, and her touch is like a butterfly kiss. "Maria," she says. "I'm with you always. Just think of me, and I'm there in your heart."

"I'm so afraid, Mama."

"You are my brave girl," she says, smiling.

"How can you say that?" I ask her. "I've always been frightened."

"Your fear makes you careful. It helped you save Nathan."

It's true. I did save my Jewish friend Nathan from certain death even though I was terrified every step of the way. The hardest choice I ever made was leaving Mama and Krystia so I could help Nathan hide in plain sight. And then once he was safe, I left him so that I could find Krystia again. My heart filled with sorrow: Mama dead, Nathan gone . . .

"Now it's time to save Krystia, and to save yourself," says Mama, her fingertips tickling my arm.

"But we're trapped," I say. "There's no way out."

Mama's eyebrows knit into a frown. "You saved Nathan even though it seemed there was no way out. You did it with careful choices, one at a time. Do what you can, Maria, instead of worrying about what you can't."

I yearn to hug her, to talk more with her, but she vanishes in a burst of light.

We went over a bump that startled me awake. I would be brave like Mama thought I was, even though there were no small things to change right now. I dried my tears, sat up straight, and as I looked around, I realized it was no longer pitch-dark inside the truck. There was a small rectangle close to the roof, now illuminated with the first rays of morning. Could that be a way to escape?

The truck must have been traveling for hours already, because we had been arrested when it was dark out and now it was beginning to be light, maybe about four in the morning. It would take hours to get back to the American camp. I wished the window had been visible when we first got in. Then maybe we could have escaped when we were still close to the Americans.

"Krystia, wake up," I said, shaking my sister's shoulder.

She lurched to a sitting position, rubbing her eyes with her knuckles. "What is it?" she asked.

"There's a window in here," I said.

She stood and stretched on tiptoes and touched the bottom of the window. "I can almost grab the bars," she said.

I wrapped my arms just below her hips and lifted her as high as I could. "Can you grab them now?"

"Got them," she said, rattling with all her might.

Krystia wasn't very heavy, but I wasn't all that strong, and I started to tremble. Krystia let go of the bars and dropped to the ground.

The red-haired boy stretched and yawned, then jumped to his feet, his eyes looking wild. "Where am I?" he shouted.

The man beside him tugged at his pant leg. "Finn, settle down. We've been arrested, and we're on our way to the Soviet zone."

The boy slid back down to a sitting position and held

his head in his hands. "And here I was hoping it was just a nightmare."

"The girls are trying to open a window, Finn," said the man as he got up from the floor. "Maybe we can escape."

The man walked over and held out his hand. "I'm Elias Reisender," he said. "And this is my son, Finn. Let me help you."

"I'm Maria Fediuk," I said. "And this is my sister, Krystia."

"Pleased to make your acquaintance." He turned to Krystia and said, "You're taller. I'll boost you."

Krystia stepped onto his hands, and I steadied her by holding her trousers from one side.

"Let me get on your shoulders," said Krystia.

Finn got up and positioned himself on the other side of Elias. Krystia climbed up the man as if he were a ladder and then gripped the bars with all her might. As she rattled them this way and that, Finn and I stood beside Elias, our arms outstretched in case she fell.

"I can't make them budge," she said. "These bars are solid."

"Can you see outside?" I asked.

"I can," she said. "But it just looks like everyplace else. Bomb and fire damage. Nothing standing."

"Are we in the country or in a town?" asked Elias.

"The country," said Krystia.

"Let me try the window," said Finn.

Krystia got down, and we helped Finn climb up to Elias's shoulders. As he gripped the bars and pulled, the sinews in his arms and neck popped out.

"I can't get them to move either," he said. He let go of the bars and dropped down to the floor, nimble as a cat.

"Even if you could have moved the bars, do you really think we would all have been able to escape?"

Sophie's voice.

I turned and glared at her. "My sister and I wouldn't even be in this truck if it wasn't for you."

"You're such a whiner," said Sophie. "Even if we could all get out that tiny window without the soldiers noticing, where would we go?"

"Back to the American camp," I said. "We could follow the road. We've been avoiding Nazis for years, so I'm sure we could avoid Soviets the same way."

"You were asleep for hours. We're probably far from the American camp," said Sophie.

"So, what's your bright suggestion for escape?" I asked her.

"Stop arguing," said Elias. "We'll have to work together if we're going to get ourselves out of this situation."

Just then, little Piotr let out a bloodcurdling shriek.

I turned to Olga, who was trying to hold Piotr on her lap, but he was flailing his arms like a windmill, hitting his mother in the chest.

Krystia put a hand under each of his armpits and gently lifted him away from his mother. "What's the matter with him?" she asked Olga in a no-nonsense voice that surprised me. The boy thrashed his arms around, but she held him at a distance so she wouldn't get hit.

"He was fidgety yesterday, probably a bad stomach from eating too quickly after not eating for so long."

The boy struggled and screamed, but Krystia kept him at arm's length, rocking him back and forth and humming under her breath. The rhythmic movement seemed to calm him enough that he stopped flailing, and so she cradled him in her arms and kept on rocking.

"Thank you for settling him," said Olga. "You look awfully young to know so much about toddlers."

"Our neighbor had a baby," said Krystia. "And I was over there a lot." She placed her hand on Piotr's forehead. "He's got a fever."

Olga sighed. "I wish I had a bit of water, or some medicine. I hate to see him suffer like this."

No one here had water or medicine, and I felt so badly for Piotr. He was too young to understand that no amount of crying would get him what he needed. And would it be any better once we got to the Soviet camp? Not likely.

"Let's sit down over there and have a look at him," said Krystia.

Olga settled against the wall and put Piotr back on her lap. He was still fretting but not as badly as before. Krystia sat beside them and gently examined Piotr.

I slumped to the ground beside Finn and Elias and marveled at this talent for helping children that my sister had apparently developed after I had escaped to Austria. I knew Krystia had some medical knowledge because she used to help Dr. Kitai, our neighbor and family friend, from time to time, but while I was at home there was no baby living beside us. Maybe she had worked for the Volksdeutsche family who had moved in after the Kitais had been forced into the ghetto.

I turned to Elias. "Do you think the Soviets were looking for a certain person, or just rounding up people they thought could be enemies?"

"I think they were looking for specific types of people," said Elias.

"I think they took Olga because her family was originally from Russia, but they were fighting against the Soviets," interjected Finn. "They took you and your sister because that one"—he jerked his head to indicate Sophie—"said you were collaborators. They were interested in her because she had false papers."

I turned to Finn and asked, "You're German, aren't you? Why were you in a refugee camp? Were the soldiers specifically looking for you and your father, and the rest of us were caught up by chance because of you?"

"We're Volksdeutsche, ethnic Germans," Finn said, his cheeks flushing. "We're originally from Bukovyna, in Ukraine."

I knew all about the Volksdeutsche. A wave of grief passed over me. Volksdeutsche were people whose families had immigrated to Ukraine from Germany centuries ago. They kept their own German customs, churches, and language, and lived in separate German communities. But during the war, the Nazis wanted to Germanize Poland and Ukraine. They did that by killing Jews in death camps and starving Poles and Ukrainians. As the native population died, the Nazis brought in Volksdeutsche settlers to replace us. I could barely say the word *Volksdeutsche* without practically spitting it out.

I turned to Elias. "What were you doing in a refugee camp in the first place?" I asked. "Couldn't you just find a friendly German family to take you two in?"

Elias sighed. "We asked at the American camp to be recognized as Dutch refugees," he said.

"But you're ethnic Germans," I said. "Why would the Americans consider you refugees?"

"We can trace part of our heritage back to the 1600s and Holland," said Elias. "We want to get out of here. I want no part of Germany or the Soviet Union."

My stomach roiled with anger at his answer. "Were you a Nazi soldier?" I asked.

"My father was in the Wehrmacht for a year," Finn replied. "And he's not a Nazi. Show her your leg, Vater."

Elias pulled up his trouser leg. From the knee down it was wooden. "Discharged for a war injury," he said.

"Nazis got injured too," I said. The words were out before I could stop them. I immediately wished I could take them back.

"It's not up to you to judge me." Elias said this not in anger but in sadness. "And if you must know, after I recovered and learned to walk on my wooden leg, I was assigned to be a policeman in Lviv. I hate the Nazis and Hitler and everything they stand for."

I had heard so many Germans claim that they didn't really believe in Hitler now that their side had lost. Was Elias like that, or did he truly not believe in Hitler's plans? I forced myself to breathe slowly and to think it through. Elias and Finn didn't choose to be Volksdeutsche, and I knew for a fact that many Volksdeutsche had been targeted and killed by the Soviets, even before the war. If Mama were here, she would tell me only Nazis view people by their race instead of their actions. So far, Finn and Elias had acted decently to us.

I took in a deep breath and let it out again, then said, "I'm sorry."

Elias extended his hand. I gripped it, and we shook.

"All is forgiven," he said. "We're in this together."

"Do you have a wife or other children?" I asked.

Elias looked down at a plain ring that he wore on his right hand, in the Volksdeutsche way. "My wife was brutally attacked by Soviet soldiers just a few weeks ago," he said. "She didn't survive. And Finn is our only child."

"Do you think the Soviets arrested you because you were a Nazi policeman, or because you were trying to claim refugee status as Dutch?" I asked.

"I have no way of knowing," said Elias.

"All I know," said Finn, "is that we've got to escape."

I nodded, but I didn't respond. His words gave me much to think about. All of us who had been captured had something to hide.

And a reason to escape.

I closed my eyes and tried to think it through, but it was such a big problem.

And then I realized that Piotr was no longer crying.

I crawled over to that side of the truck to see what was going on. Piotr was stretched out beside Olga, resting his head on Krystia's rolled-up jacket. Olga caressed his tear-streaked cheek, and my heart ached for him. It was scary enough for all of us to be captives, but this little boy was so innocent and vulnerable. What crime did the Soviets think this toddler had committed?

"Try to keep him in this position," said Krystia. "I think he has an earache. Angled like this, if there's fluid in there, it can drain."

Olga reached over and brushed Krystia's cheek. "Thank you. I was at my wit's end."

"I'm glad I could help," said Krystia.

She stood up and stretched, then came over to where I was and slumped down beside me.

"Maybe we should all get some sleep," she said.

I closed my eyes, but sleep seemed far away. Others had no problem though, because after a few minutes, one person's breathing took on the rhythm of sleep, then another's. The truck careened over bumps and curves, bringing us all closer to our uncertain future. Finally sleep came to me as well.

CHAPTER FIVE–
SHOES
KRYSTIA

Even though I was exhausted, I couldn't sleep. Maria had finally drifted off and so had almost everyone else. But Olga was awake, and she was weeping.

I crawled over to her and Piotr. The light through the window was faint, but I could see the remnants of tears in the corners of the little boy's eyes and the flush of fever on his cheeks. He was sleeping deeply though, and I hoped he felt a bit better when he woke. Olga had her arms wrapped around her knees, and her shoulders shook with emotion. I put my hand on her back and gently rubbed.

"We'll get out of this," I said.

She looked up at me. Her face was mottled with tears, but she looked angry, not sad. "Such an easy thing for you to say," she whispered, "when you don't have a child."

She was right. It wasn't the same. Piotr would never be able to run away from soldiers. He didn't know how to be quiet or when to stay hidden. And he could be used as a weapon against his mother. Against any of us, really. His pain from a mere earache was nothing compared to what a Soviet soldier might do to him. But I didn't want to talk to her about that. If I said it out loud, it wouldn't make it better, so I changed the subject.

"How did you end up here in the first place?" I asked.

She took a deep breath and stretched her legs out straight beside my own: four feet lined up in a row in front of us; mine bare, covered with dirt and calluses, hers encased in heavy leather shoes that had seen better days.

"It's a long story," she said. "But I'll tell you the short version. During the Russian Revolution in 1917, my father joined the White Army, fighting for a democratic government. The Red Army was fighting for a communist dictatorship. They won. The first thing they did was kill those who disagreed with them. Our family fled to England."

"That's interesting history," I said. "But what's that got to do with this war?"

"We still want a democracy in Russia," said Olga. "My husband enlisted to defeat the Soviets."

"He fought with the Nazis?" I asked.

32

"He fought in the German army, but just to defeat the Soviet dictatorship."

"But why are you here?"

"Wives and children came with their husbands—it kept up their morale—but I got separated from my husband and the group. I found out that he's in a British camp and thought we'd be reunited, but then this happened . . ." She lifted her arms to indicate the truck, then let them fall limply to her side.

I squeezed her hand but didn't say anything. What encouragement could I possibly give her?

"I've seen what the Red Army does to people who fight for democracy," said Olga in a flat voice. "I do not want my child to have a slow and painful death, and I do not want to be tortured and risk giving information that could hurt my husband and our friends."

We sat side by side for a long moment, and I thought about how crucial it was that we all escaped, especially for Piotr's sake.

I thought Olga was asleep, but then she spoke. "Our feet are about the same size. If anything happens to me, you get my shoes."

I didn't speak right away because I was afraid I'd just sob. I squeezed her hand. Finally I said, "If something happens to you, I'll look after Piotr."

She nodded but kept her eyes on her son. A tear rolled down the side of her face.

I took a deep breath and said, "If something happens to me, can you please look after my sister?"

She turned to me and patted my cheek. "I will, child."

The truck rumbled on. Sleep enveloped me.

I woke with a jolt.

Sunlight stabbed my eyes; the truck was at a standstill.

"Out, all of you," said Vlad.

I tried to get to my feet, but the bright light blinded me and I nearly tripped over someone. An arm looped through my elbow.

"I've got you," Maria said.

She tried to guide me as best she could as we jumped down from the truck together, but I was still blind from the sunlight and couldn't see the ground. My bare feet hit sharp stones. Pain shot up my legs, my knees buckled, and my face planted into gravel.

"Up, now," shouted Misha.

He poked my back with what felt like the tip of a rifle. Maria pulled me to my feet, and my eyes finally began to adapt to the bright sunlight. We were in farmland with bombed-out barns and houses. In a pasture nearby, there was a bloated corpse of a cow that buzzed with flies, and the fields and gravel road were peppered with huge bomb craters and an explosion of blood-smeared chicken feathers. The road was blocked with rubble.

Was this our opportunity to escape?

CHAPTER SIX— RUN!
MARIA

The two Red Army soldiers, Misha and Vlad, stood in front of our sorry group, rifles poised.

"Don't even think about trying to escape," said Misha. "Your job here is to clear the road so we can continue on."

It was a treacherous job dismantling the rubble pile one brick at a time with my bare hands. Many of the bricks had shattered, leaving sharp, jagged edges, and the concrete had split into heavy chunks. I could carry bricks myself if I was careful with them, but the chunks of concrete were too heavy. Depending on the size of the chunk, it took two or three of us to carry each one out of the way. It took hours to clear the worst of it. As we worked, I tried to get an idea of the countryside, looking for a place that we might run to. The cow pasture itself was too exposed, but beyond it was a hilly area covered with bushes; from what I could see it looked like the best place to hide if I got the chance.

I caught Krystia's eye as she limped past me, the final bricks in each hand. I pretended to brush some hair out of my eye but pointed toward the hilly area. She looked that way and nodded so slightly that only I could see.

"No dawdling," said Vlad. He pushed my shoulder. "Time to get back in the truck."

I turned toward him but cast my eyes to the ground. "How much farther is the journey, comrade?" I asked him.

He seemed to like it that I called him comrade because when he answered, his tone was less harsh. "A few more hours, depending on the road," he said.

"We've all been traveling for so long. Would it be possible for us to have some water and perhaps a chance to relieve ourselves before we get back in the truck?" I asked.

"There's no water," he said. "But I guess you should have a chance to pee." He shaded his eyes with his hand, scanning the area for a good spot. "You can go behind that bush, one at a time," he said, pointing to a sorry-looking shrub not far from the dead cow. "Don't try to escape. I'll shoot you without a moment's hesitation."

I went first, and as I squatted in the privacy of the bush, I wondered how we might distract the two soldiers.

But when I finished and stepped away from the bush, Vlad was watching me.

Krystia was next in line, and when she was finished, we sat side by side on the edge of the truck, our legs dangling. Elias, Finn, and Sophie took their turns behind the bush and then came back. Elias sat beside us, as did Finn, but Sophie clambered into the truck and slumped down in a far dark corner by herself.

The two soldiers stood together about halfway between the truck and the bush, their rifles pointed to the ground. I could tell they were both keeping an eye on us, but they were also chatting.

When it was Olga's turn, instead of going to the bush, she approached me and Krystia, balancing Piotr on her hip with one hand. In her other hand she carried her shoes. She set the shoes on Krystia's lap and whispered, "Put the shoes on quickly, now. I'm giving you and Maria a chance to escape."

How was she giving us a chance to escape? And why had she given her shoes to Krystia? Her words made no sense. Krystia seemed confused as well. She tried to give the shoes back, but Olga thrust them back into her hands.

"*Now*," hissed Olga. "*Put. On. The. Shoes!*"

Krystia, her face tense with emotion, slipped on both shoes. They seemed to fit her perfectly, but I couldn't understand why Olga would give them away. My own shoes were nearly falling apart, but they were more precious than gold.

Olga's shoulders relaxed once she saw the shoes on my sister's feet. She grabbed Krystia's arm and said, "Thank you for your kindness. Good luck to you and your sister. I'll see you in heaven."

Krystia's face went pale. She gripped Olga's hand. "Don't do it," she said.

But Olga shrugged her off.

Misha came up to us. "Get inside," he said. "It's time to go."

Right then, Olga wrapped both her arms tightly around Piotr and bolted.

I stood in shock as she hobbled barefoot toward the hill. She'd taken a dozen steps or more by the time the soldiers seemed to understand what was happening.

"Stop!" Misha shouted. "I'll shoot."

"But she has a child!" I screamed. "You might shoot him by mistake."

The soldier didn't acknowledge my words. He aimed his rifle at Olga's back and pulled the trigger. A loud shot rang out.

The bullet missed Olga by a hair, but it seemed to startle her. She stumbled, but found her footing, and kept on running. Piotr flailed and screamed.

Misha dropped his rifle and ran after Olga. When he got close enough, he drew out his pistol and fired.

Olga crumpled and fell, right on top of Piotr. Her back blossomed in red.

Misha pulled Olga's body off Piotr's. A blotch of red covered his chest as well. One of the bullets must have gone right through Olga and hit the boy.

Krystia cried, "You killed a child!"

Vlad, who was standing close to us, looked at Krystia with a flash of anger, then he smashed the butt of his rifle into the side of her head. I grabbed her just in time to break her fall.

"Back in the truck, now!" shouted the soldier.

Elias and Finn helped me lift Krystia inside. We were barely all in before the doors slammed shut. The truck began to move.

CHAPTER SEVEN-
SOVIET ZONE
KRYSTIA

My skull was a bundle of pain.

It got worse when the truck bumped over a hole in the road. Maria nestled my head in her lap and, while I appreciated the gesture, her legs were too bony to make a good pillow. But she kept my head from lolling back and forth as the truck swayed, and that was a good thing. I tried to sit up, but a burst of stars appeared behind my eyes, and I thought I was going to throw up. Maria grabbed me by the shoulders and slowly eased me into a sitting position.

"You need to be careful," she said. "You were out for maybe an hour. I just got the bleeding stopped, and you don't want to open up the wound again."

My hand flew to my scalp, where I felt a strip of cloth wrapped around where it hurt the most.

"How are your feet?" she asked.

I had landed on those sharp stones, yet strangely my feet didn't bother me. I looked down at them and nearly gasped when I saw Olga's shoes. And then I remembered: Olga was dead, and so was Piotr. How could Olga possibly think that I would use her death as part of an escape plan? Did she think I would use her suffering for my benefit? The thought sent chills through me. What kind of person ran away while a friend was being shot at? I looked back down at my feet and regarded Olga's well-worn but sturdy shoes. They were in remarkable condition considering how far she'd walked in them, carrying her son, trying to protect him.

Protect him.

Why did she want to be dead? Want her son dead?

Tears splashed down my face. I wished I could turn back time. I wished I could grab Olga and stop her from killing herself and Piotr. It was my fault that she was dead, and these shoes were proof that I benefited from her death.

I reached to remove one of the shoes.

"Leave them," said Maria.

"But it makes me feel awful wearing these," I said.

"Olga wanted you to have them," said Maria. "Honor her memory and wear them. It's all that we can do for her now."

I wanted nothing more than to kick these shoes off and throw them out the window, but I knew that Maria was right. These shoes were all that remained of Olga. They were a gift from her heart, to help me survive. I had to wear them in memory of her and Piotr. And if we survived? Maybe I could find her husband and give him back these shoes. I could let him know how his wife and child had died.

The truck motored on, and our small group of prisoners remained silent, clearly wrapped in private thoughts and fears. But then Sophie spoke.

"Olga had to do it," she said.

"Why do you say that?" I asked.

"I was stationed in Czechoslovakia practically to the end of the war," said Sophie. "We all heard about what those Russians in the German army were up to."

"Olga told me," I said. "They wanted to bring democracy to Russia."

Sophie grunted. "If only it were that simple," she said. "They were traitors to everybody except themselves."

Sophie was the last person I wanted to have a conversation with, but I couldn't stop myself from asking, "What are you talking about?"

"They may have been in the German army, but they weren't loyal," she said. "They assisted the Czech underground army to defeat the Nazis in Prague. They were fighting the Nazis and the Soviets. Can you imagine what would happen to her and Piotr if the Soviets got her to their camp? They'd torture her son in front of her to get information from her, and then they'd kill her. I've heard that entire families have committed suicide to avoid that fate."

Sophie's words were like a dagger in my heart. Our situation was almost identical to Olga's. Maria and I were anti-Nazi *and* anti-Soviet, and we wanted to live in a democracy. What would the Soviets do to us if they found out about our work helping to rescue Jews from the Nazis and working with the Ukrainian Underground to defeat both dictatorships?

I nudged Maria with my elbow, then whispered in her ear. "No matter what, we can't say anything about the Ukrainian Insurgent Army," I told her. "Even if they threaten to kill us."

She squeezed my hand and said, "Death would be preferable to betraying our friends."

As the journey continued, the monotonous motion of the truck lulled us all into a sort of trance. And then, the truck stopped.

The doors opened. Misha stood there, his cap on crooked and his hair askew, looking like he just woke up. But he held a rifle, plus the pistol, and he pointed them both at us.

"Out!" he said.

Elias was the first one out of the truck, and he stood at the door to assist me. I was so stiff and sore that I felt like an old woman, so I was grateful when his hand gripped my arm as he helped me down.

I took in a huge gulp of cool air and tried to focus, but my head still throbbed from being smashed by the butt of Vlad's rifle. Once my vision stopped swirling, I realized we were standing in front of a bombed-out town.

Misha pointed to the rubble-filled roadway that went through the center of it and said, "That's where we're going.

"We'll need to walk through this town to get to our destination," he added as he gazed sternly at each of us one by one. His eyes rested on me the longest. "Don't even think about trying to escape," he said.

Misha and Vlad divided us into two groups; Maria, Sophie, and I were supposed to walk up front with Misha guarding us, while Finn and Elias walked behind with Vlad's gun trained on them.

My head hurt and I was barely awake, but even so I was grateful to finally be out in the open instead of in the back of that stuffy dark truck. As I walked through town in Olga's sturdy shoes, I was mesmerized by the magnitude of the desolation. We walked past what must have been at one time a four-story building; now it had only one wall remaining. It made me gasp to look at it, wondering if it would fall down on top of us. All around were huge pyramids of blasted brick and stone, and most of the buildings were destroyed right down to the foundation. Men and women walked through all this rubble, industriously maneuvering shovels, pickaxes, and wheelbarrows, clearing away the destruction one brick at a time. I was pretty sure they were German because they weren't skinny enough to be former slave laborers or camp survivors. Was this the Soviet zone?

None of the locals looked up when we passed. Were they afraid of being arrested by the Soviets too? Or maybe they were so used to seeing Soviet soldiers with prisoners that there was no reason to take note of us.

I kept my eyes fixed on the ground so I wouldn't trip in the rubble, and as we walked I saw glimpses of what life had been like before the destruction. Had the broken tube of red lipstick glittering in the sunlight beside a brick belonged to an entertainer in a theater? Or maybe the lipstick had been a gift from a husband to his new wife. A solitary white ladies' glove was caught on a shard of glass, and as it blew in the wind it looked like a small flag of surrender. A block or so after the glove, the dizziness nearly got the better of me, and I almost fell onto a dented bird-cage, but Maria steadied me just in time.

We walked through to the end of the town, and the road opened up onto the countryside. The road became more passable because the blasted-out buildings were farther apart, but there were the usual giant bomb-holes in the road that you could break a leg on if you didn't watch where you were going. There were also sharp shards of stone and glass beneath our feet with almost every footstep. Every time I felt a crunch of glass or rubble under Olga's shoe, I thought of the people who had lived here before the war. Maybe a family with young children and a cow? They had been filled with hope for the future, like we all had. Where were they now? Scattered across the continent? Or maybe all dead. My heart broke at the thought of so many lives cut short.

Olga's shoes protected me from the shrapnel and glass, and I felt almost like she was watching over us. I sang a quiet "Vichnaya Pamyat" under my breath for her and Piotr. Maria walked beside me, and as she clasped my hand to steady me, she sang the hymn of eternal life along with me.

For those few moments as I walked with my sister on the open road in the fresh air, singing in quiet harmony our holy song, I felt at peace. I felt almost free. For a brief moment I forgot about Sophie walking beside us and Misha's gun at our backs.

How I savored this last bit of freedom.

"I am so thirsty," whispered Maria.

That jolted me to the present. I tried to swallow, but my mouth was like paper.

All too soon, the road led us up a hill and around a corner. There was no fence, and no wall, but guards blocked the road. Was this where the Soviet zone began?

CHAPTER EIGHT—
YAWNING BLACKNESS
MARIA

Vlad walked up to one of the border guards and showed him some papers. The guards stepped aside and gestured for us all to continue down the road. As we walked past them, I was confused but also relieved. If it was this easy to walk into the Soviet zone, wouldn't it be just as easy to walk out again? Couldn't we blend in with the civilians who were clearing out rubble and make our escape?

I gave Krystia's hand a squeeze and said, "I think it's all going to be fine."

She squeezed my hand back, but she didn't look at me.

The road took us through the main part of yet another ruined town. Like everywhere, there were few buildings left standing, and people were busily cleaning up the damage. There was one key difference though. In addition to the people who looked like they probably lived here, there were also prisoners, supervised by Red Army soldiers, who were doing some of the heaviest work. But they were alive. And they were still here in Germany, not sent to a slave camp in Siberia.

"Krystia, look at them," I whispered in Ukrainian.

"What about them?" she asked. "Maybe soon we'll be just like those prisoners."

"But they're here, not shipped somewhere far away," I said.

"But for how long?" said Krystia.

She had a point. "We have to escape soon, then . . ."

"No talking!" shouted Misha, jabbing my back with the butt of his rifle. "I may not know much Ukrainian, but I've learned the word—*втікати*—escape. You're not escaping on my watch, so forget about it."

As Misha prodded us on, I was overwhelmed by how huge our problem was. Even if both Krystia and I managed to get away from the soldiers, where would we hide? All around us, buildings were in ruins. Even the people who lived here must struggle to find food and a place to sleep. If we got away from the soldiers, would any of these people help us, or would they turn their eyes away, not wanting to get involved?

I walked in silence, wrapped up in my own thoughts

but stepping carefully so I didn't slice open my shoes on shattered glass or sharp shards of brick. I was fairly sure that these Red Army soldiers would be just as likely to shoot me as to give me first aid. I kept a firm grip on Krystia's hand, guiding her because she was still dizzy from her injury, and my eyes scanned the ground, watching where to step. And that's when I saw a frayed tuft of sky-blue cloth clinging to the edge of a ruined wicker basket. It was the exact color of Mama's favorite blouse.

The bit of cloth looked like it had been from someone's clothing. Was that person now dead, like Mama, and this cloth was all that was left of them? My heart filled with sorrow. I missed Mama, but I also mourned for all the people who had been caught up in this horrible war. As I stepped over the wicker basket, I grabbed the piece of cloth. I held it to my heart, and it was as if Mama were there with me, her spirit within that bit of blue cloth.

As we walked, I was overcome with sadness. Mama dead. Aunts, uncles dead. Neighbors, friends, and cousins all dead. Our house, our town, and our country all in ruins. Some killed by Nazis, some by Soviets. Two terrible dictatorships. With just the Nazis gone but the Soviets still around, how could we even say that the war was over? I was so afraid.

But as I clasped that little piece of blue, Mama's voice filled my mind.

51

"*Do what you can, Maria, instead of worrying about what you can't.*"

And then I remembered her words from my dream:

"*Your fear makes you careful. It helped you save Nathan.*"

She was right about that. I did it with small choices, one at a time.

Now I would need to do the same thing for myself and Krystia.

While I knew it was true, it was also frustrating, considering the circumstances. Here I was, a prisoner of the Soviets, starving, thirsty, and tired, with an injured sister I had to guide along so she wouldn't fall.

"*But what can you do that others can't?*" said Mama's voice in my head.

I squeezed the cloth. *Nothing, Mama,* I thought. *I'm useless.*

But then I remembered that it was because I was watching my steps and guiding my sister that I found the blue cloth. What other things might I see because I must look down instead of forward? I scanned the ground as I guided Krystia.

We walked and walked, up pyramids of rubble and down the other side. Around an upended baby carriage covered in dust, nearly falling into a gaping hole filled with muddy water. I almost jumped in shock when I saw a pair of eyes staring back out at me from what I thought was just a pile of rubble.

I blinked a few times before I understood what I was seeing—a person in what remained of a house, now just an intact cellar beneath a pile of blasted bricks and stones. Could a person live in a place like that?

Now that I knew what I was looking for, I kept my eyes peeled for more people living in cellars camouflaged by rubble. We stepped past an openly visible basement with the rubble cleared away. A woman sitting at a kitchen table in that basement looked up at me and nodded. My nose wrinkled at the scent of frying onion, and then I spied a tendril of smoke. Someone was cooking on a wood or coal stove, hidden in this rubble. The normalcy amid the ruins was jarring.

But where *were* we? It was impossible to know how many twists and turns the truck had taken to get to this place from the American camp. Even the street signs had been bombed.

The ground became more walkable when we got to the edge of the town, so I was finally able to look forward instead of always down. Judging by the size of the properties, we were in an area that must have been where wealthy people had once lived. The houses themselves were all destroyed except one, a huge stone-and-stucco mansion with extensive grounds, all surrounded by a tall stone wall. I could only see the top floor above the wall, but it looked miraculously undamaged. Even most of the surrounding wall was intact, although an oak tree on one side of it had split in two, and the part of the wall closest to the tree had lost a few stones. The damage had been hastily repaired with bricks and concrete, and either the Soviets or the Nazis had topped the entire wall with coils of barbed wire.

Was this going to be our prison? I gazed up and squinted to get a better look at the top of the house. There was a series of round stone towers with stained glass windows at the very top, and the windows had no bars. But even if we were put in one of those rooms and managed to break a window, how would we be able to scale the wall and get over the barbed wire? Krystia caught my eye, and I'm pretty sure she was thinking the same thing.

The double-doored entrance in the wall looked like a more promising place to escape because there was no barbed wire there. Unfortunately, it was patrolled by Red Army soldiers with machine guns. Did they take breaks or walk the perimeter the way the Nazis did in the ghettos? Maybe there was a way to get out if we timed it just right.

"Stop where you are," said one of the Red Army guards, pointing his machine gun at us.

Misha stepped forward and handed the guard our

papers. "These are criminals that we've apprehended from the American camp in Karlsfeld," he said.

Criminals? I rolled that word over in my mind.

"You can go through," said the guard, lowering his weapon.

They opened the double doors, and we stepped through.

Once inside the courtyard, we walked single file toward the mansion, and I kept my eyes on the ground. My heart sank as we paused at the entrance to the mansion itself because I realized that this would not be a good route of escape. The original door was nothing more than wooden shards on the ground; it had been replaced with a movable barbed wire barricade.

Like the stone wall surrounding the property, the mansion entrance was protected by guards with machine guns. They pulled the barricade aside, and our two soldiers pushed us through with the tips of their rifles.

We stepped inside. This mansion looked like it was all business, not anyone's residence anymore. The chandelier still hung from above, but it was covered in dust and most of the crystals were missing. All along the walls were discolored rectangles where artwork and portraits had hung.

There were four desks, two on each side of the otherwise spartan reception area. Each of the desks had a typewriter, a phone, and stacks of paper, but only one had a person sitting at it: a woman in an embroidered blouse who was typing at an energetic pace. She didn't look up as we walked in, and our soldier escorts walked past her as they nudged us toward a wide wooden staircase that was scraped and scuffed from army boots.

Instead of going up the staircase, though, we were guided to a sturdy wooden door behind it. One of the soldiers pulled it open, then shoved the five of us into a yawning blackness.

CHAPTER NINE–
A PRAYER
KRYSTIA

I felt myself falling into the blackness, so I stretched my arms out to break the fall. The last thing I needed was to smack down on my face again or to open up the wound on my scalp. Just then, hands grasped my shoulders, steadying me, stopping the fall.

"I've got you," said Maria.

Her words almost made me cry. I was so grateful for my steady, sturdy little sister. All those months when she was hiding in the Reich helping Nathan, and I stayed back in Viteretz helping Mama, my heart had ached with her absence. We did what we had to then, not only to stay alive but to help our friends. But we were a team, and we could do so much together. We would figure out a way to escape from this place—whatever this place was. Clutching each other, my sister and I moved in the darkness together until we bumped into a wall. I brushed my hands over the wall and whacked my knuckle against a set of bars.

I moved back to where the wall was smooth and leaned against it. I slid down onto the floor. Maria looped her hand around my elbow and slid down with me. She grabbed one of my hands and put a piece of cloth in it. "I found this," she said.

"A piece of cloth?" I asked, not really understanding why she was so excited about it.

"A piece of sky-blue cloth," Maria said. "The exact color of Mama's favorite blouse."

I held it up to my face and felt the smooth weave. I breathed in deeply and savored the faint scent of sweat and berries. Even without seeing the blue of the cloth it already reminded me of Mama. My throat caught in sorrow. No one could ever be as brave as Mama was. She outsmarted the invaders, the killers, winning again and again. But in the end, they caught her. How I wished I could have saved her, but in the end I was powerless. My mind filled with the image of her corpse swinging from that scaffold in the center of our town. I held the cloth to my face once more. Mama was gone, that was true. But her spirit lived on in me and in Maria. It was a fighting spirit.

"Thank you for finding this," I said to my sister as I

handed the cloth back to her. "You're right. Even without being able to see its color, the feel and the scent remind me of Mama."

Just then there was a loud click from right outside our door. Suddenly the room was filled with light. I squinted from the brightness. We were in a room that at one time may have been an office or a bedroom but had been modified into a holding cell. The metal bars that my hand had brushed up against covered a large boarded-up window in the corner of the room. Finn and Elias sat beside us on the bare wooden floor, while Sophie sat on the opposite side of the room, her arms wrapped around her knees and a scowl on her face.

The room itself had no furniture, but in one corner at Sophie's end of the room, there was an enamel toilet without a seat.

The woman in the embroidered blouse stood just inside the door—she must have turned on the light. "You'll get something to eat shortly, and after that we'll sort you all out." She slipped back out the door and closed it with a firm click that was followed by the sound of metal scraping metal—maybe a dead bolt? Her words were the most encouraging I'd heard since our arrest.

I walked over to the toilet and peered inside. No water. I jiggled the handle. It didn't work. How embarrassing it would be to have to use this broken toilet, here in this open room, with Maria, Finn, Elias, and Sophie looking on!

I walked to the window, pushing at the bars here and there to see if any were loose. I rattled the door too, but it was solid.

"You can't get out of here," said Sophie.

"It never hurts to check." I walked back to my spot between Maria, Finn, and Elias and slid down to the floor.

"How long do you think they'll hold us here?" asked Finn, sitting cross-legged beside his father.

"They'll probably leave us here until we rot," answered Sophie from the other side of the room.

"When you were a Hitler Girl, did you win any badges?" asked Maria.

Sophie sat up straight and jutted out her chin. "I was very successful in the Jugend."

"You certainly didn't win any badges for a pleasant personality," said Maria.

Her comment made me laugh out loud, but Sophie jumped to her feet and stomped over to Maria.

"Take that back," she said, "or I'll beat you."

Maria stood up and locked eyes with Sophie. "Such a pleasant personality," she said. "Did you get a badge for fighting, at least?"

Sophie balled her hands into fists, and it looked like she was about to punch Maria, but Elias stood up—surprisingly nimbly for someone with a wooden leg—and held both of Sophie's forearms. "We're all friends here," he said. "Let's not waste our energy by fighting each other."

Sophie tried to pull away from Elias, but his grip was firm. "Why are you telling me this?" she said. "Maria started it."

"Don't," said Elias, in a voice that trembled with controlled rage. "You denounced both of those girls to the Soviet militia, and by doing so, you caused them to be arrested and you caused yourself to be arrested as well. Since then, you've been sour and unpleasant. If anyone should be on their best behavior, it's you."

"Being nice won't get me out of this mess," said Sophie.

Elias let go of her, and I noticed that there were red marks on each of her forearms where he had gripped her. She walked back to her spot on the other side of the room and slumped to the ground.

Elias turned to Maria and said, "Don't provoke her."

"If you knew all that she did to me and to her own family, you might think differently," said Maria.

"And who made you the judge?" asked Elias. He pointed at Sophie but looked at Maria. "God is her judge, not you. And she has to live with her own conscience."

"I also have to live with the things that she's done," said Maria.

"Grow up," said Sophie. "I treated you better than a Slav deserves."

Just then the door opened, and the woman in the embroidered blouse walked in. Behind her was an elderly woman in a dusty dress with her hair wrapped in a kerchief. She was carrying a covered metal pot that was the diameter of a dinner plate. Hooked on one of her fingers was a metal cup.

"Excuse me, Galina," the old woman said in Russian as she tried to step past the woman without bumping her. She placed the pot on the floor, then set the cup beside it. "You'll have to share the cup," she said to us in German. "This is all I have to spare."

As she backed out of the room, she regarded each one of us with a sorrowful expression. "May God be with each of you," she said.

"God," said Galina, rolling her eyes. "I hope none of you believe in those fables anymore." She and the old woman left.

As soon as the door closed, Sophie lunged toward the pot and grabbed the cup. She was about to dip it into the pot when Elias said in a firm voice, "Stop."

"We can all have a turn," said Sophie. "But someone has to start."

"We're all starving," said Finn. "And we have to make sure that we all get equal amounts." He turned to look at Elias. "Vater should serve it."

"No," said Elias. "There's one of us here who's been brave and has tried to help others."

He turned to me.

"Krystia, will you please serve us our food?"

His words made me want to weep. But even more, I just wanted to eat. I crawled over to the pot and removed the lid.

Soup.

Watery soup.

In fact, soup so watery that I could see the bottom of the pot. I picked up the cup and dipped it in, swirling the concoction about. There was no meat in it, but there were a few chunks of vegetable and some pieces of potato too. How would I manage to fairly divide this into five equal portions? I filled a cup with the lukewarm liquid and passed it to Finn.

"Take one sip," I said. "Then pass it around."

Finn took it from my hands with reverence and care. He took a sip, then looked around, frowning, trying to decide who to give it to next. In an act of conciliation, he stood up and walked over to Sophie. He squatted down until he was at eye level with her and then handed her the cup.

Sophie blinked back tears. "Thank you," she said, taking one small sip.

Sophie stood and walked over to Maria. She knelt in front of her and proffered the cup. "Here," she said.

Maria looked at her in surprise. She took the cup and swallowed her sip without saying a word to Sophie. I figured that sharing the cup without an argument was almost as good as an apology.

Maria served Elias next, and then it was my turn.

The soup had no salt, and there was a faint taste of rot, but that first mouthful was nothing short of heavenly. I held the liquid on my dry cracked tongue as long as I could and reveled in its sustenance. When I finally swallowed it down, it felt like a salve on my parched throat.

We continued to share the soup one sip at a time, making sure that each one of us got the exact same morsels of vegetable and potato. When the pot was empty, there was one lump of potato left at the bottom.

"I need to divide this in five," I said. "But I have nothing to cut it with."

"This will work," said Elias, slipping off his wedding

ring and passing it to me. The heft of that ring was like a flash of memory, but I brushed it aside for now.

I used the edge of his ring to cut the bit of potato and was pleased to see that I was able to divide it exactly. We each reached in and took our morsel between our thumbs and index fingers. Just before I popped mine into my mouth, Maria held up her hand to stop us.

"We should give our thanks for this food," she said.

"Nazis don't believe in prayer," said Elias. "And neither do the Soviets. But I'm neither a Nazi nor a Soviet, and I would love to thank God for this food."

Finn nodded in agreement, and so did I. Sophie said nothing. She popped her bit of potato into her mouth and swallowed it down. The rest of us said our words of thanks, then solemnly placed that last bit of potato onto our tongues. The watery soup revived me in more ways than I could count. I looked around our cell, at my dear sister, Maria, at Finn, Elias, and even Sophie. It wasn't just Maria and I who had to escape.

We were all in this together.

But could we all get out together? I hoped and prayed that we could.

A wave of exhaustion washed over me. My head still hurt, and my body ached. I curled into a ball on the floor and closed my eyes. Feeling the heft of Elias's wedding ring had reminded me of my own father's ring. My mind filled with an image of Tato in bed, just before he died of lung cancer. Maria was so little back then, she probably had almost no memory of him, but for me, Tato loomed large. I had sat on his bed and gripped his hand so tightly that his plain gold wedding band dug into my palm.

"You are my eldest daughter, Krystia," he had said, pulling me toward him and kissing me on the forehead. "And I am grateful for your strength."

"But I'm just a young girl," I had said. "How can I be strong?"

"Some will assume you're stupid because you're Ukrainian," he said. "Others will think you're weak because you're young, and a girl. But their prejudice gives you power."

"But how?" I asked.

"Because you can do what they don't expect."

As I lay curled up on the holding-cell floor, I thought about my father's words. What he'd said had certainly been true when our town was occupied by the Nazis. Their assumptions gave me invisibility. I had spirited food into the ghetto under their noses. I'd acted as a courier between prisoners in the ghetto and insurgents in the woods.

And what of the Soviets? What were their prejudices against people like me? And how could I use their prejudice as my strength?

I sat back up and took a deep breath. We would get through this. I knew it.

CHAPTER TEN–
SOFT TORTURE
MARIA

The soup tasted horrible, but it took the edge off my hunger. And after I swallowed that last bit of potato I was overwhelmed with exhaustion. Was it day or night? It was hard to tell. Our prison had a boarded-up window and was artificially lit with a single light bulb. I knew that I should stay awake. At any moment, the door might open and our circumstances could change, but my eyes would not stay open.

Krystia had curled into a ball on the floor, and I thought she was sound asleep, but she stretched out and sat up, looking more refreshed than I would have thought possible after such a short nap.

"You sleep now, and I'll sleep again later," said Krystia, yawning. "I'll wake you in an hour or so."

I curled up onto the floor, using my jacket as a pillow,

and must have fallen asleep instantly. And dreamed . . .

Mama, wearing her blue blouse.

She holds that last piece of potato in the palm of her hand. She takes off her wedding ring and holds it up so I can see, and then she uses it like a knife, slicing through the potato, making five equal pieces.

"Break your problem into smaller pieces," she says.

I reach out to touch her, but she's like the mist of breath in winter, and my hand goes right through her. "Please, Mama, stay with me."

"I'm with you always," she says.

Mama disappears . . .

I tossed and turned, not fully asleep but not quite awake either. Anxious thoughts ran through my mind in a loop. Cutting problems into bits like cutting a potato. What problem had I solved lately? None at all. I couldn't stop us from being caught by the Soviets. I didn't manage to find a way to escape while we were traveling. Now we were in a locked room in a house that was under armed guard. How could I break this huge problem into smaller pieces?

I was wrapped in a cold blanket of failure.

I jerked awake, trembling uncontrollably.

Not from failure, but because I was freezing. My feet felt like blocks of ice, and my hands and arms were numb with cold. I stood up and stomped my feet, trying to get the blood flowing.

"Are you all right?" asked Krystia. She stood up and wove her warm fingers through mine. "You're like ice," she said, taking off her jacket and draping it over my shoulders. The jacket had some of her warmth still in it, and I started to thaw out.

I spread my jacket out on the floor and sat on it, wrapping the sleeves around my legs. Krystia cuddled up beside me. Slowly, I began to feel a bit less cold.

I must have drifted off again, cozy in the warmth of the two jackets, but then I woke when I felt Krystia shivering.

"It's your turn to get warm," I said, draping a jacket over her shoulders. She smiled gratefully.

I looked at our fellow captives to see how they were faring. Elias and Finn were side by side, arms wrapped tightly around each other, and they seemed warm enough. Sophie was another matter. Her arms were wrapped around her knees, but her body shook with cold.

"Come on," I said to Krystia. "We need to share some body heat."

Sophie looked surprised as I sat down on one side of her and Krystia sat down on the other. Krystia took my jacket and draped it over Sophie's knees. We each grabbed one of Sophie's hands, warming them up with our own.

Gradually she stopped trembling. "Thank you," she said.

"We're in this together," said Krystia.

Sophie opened her mouth to say something but then closed it. From the corner of my eye I could see her blinking back some tears. Finally she took a deep breath and sighed. "I owe both of you an apology," she said.

I felt like saying something sarcastic but stopped myself, just in time. Was our mutual hatred part of the big problem? Maybe not, but it was something I could change, just like Mama said. After everything Sophie had done to me at the Huber farm, I couldn't bring myself to be nice yet, but I could try not to be rude.

In my silence, Krystia replied, "Your apology is accepted."

"Really?" said Sophie. "Just like that?"

"We can't turn back time," said Krystia. "And it takes guts to apologize. So yes, just like that."

Sophie's whole body seemed to soften. She looked my way. "I know you hate me."

"*Hate* is a strong word," said Krystia.

I couldn't stand it any longer. "*Hate* may be a strong word," I said, leaning forward so I could see my sister's eyes. "But it's close to how I feel about Sophie."

"I'm sitting right here," said Sophie. "And I'd prefer that you didn't talk about me as if I wasn't."

"Okay, Sophie," I said, looking straight at her. "Do you want me to list all the reasons why you're not my favorite person?"

"I know the reasons," Sophie replied. "But all those things, like me ordering you around, locking you in the cellar, tattling on you when you ate too much food for a Slav, I had to do them. It's not like I enjoyed it."

"I think you did enjoy it," I said. "I think you enjoyed tormenting your poor mother and grandparents and reporting them to Blockleiter Schutt. I think you enjoyed getting more food than the rest of your family. And I think you particularly enjoyed all the power you got as a Jugend."

Sophie's shoulders slumped, and she let out a deep sigh. "I did enjoy it for a little while," she said. "But the Jugends didn't give me a chance to think things through. The Nazis made it the law for Aryan kids to join once they reached age ten, and then they told us their lies every day."

"So, you're saying you don't believe all that stuff now?" I demanded.

Sophie didn't reply right away, but after a few moments she said, "I don't know what to believe anymore."

"How did you end up in a refugee camp?" asked Krystia. "Couldn't you have just gone home?"

"I did go home," said Sophie. "Or what was left of it."

She turned to me and said, "I got there just after Krystia found you and the two of you left."

"Why didn't you stay there?" I asked.

"I wanted to," she said. "Our farm had been ruined by bombs and looting. Mutter needed me, and I was so sick of the war." She wiped a tear from the corner of her eye. "I hung up my uniform and vowed to help my family get back on their feet."

I did have a bit of sympathy for Sophie's family, who had shown me some kindness. But Sophie's story also made me think about my own home. The Soviets pillaged it first, then the Nazis came in and shot the Jews, then gave their homes and clothing to the Aryans they brought in. Nazis said people like me were "Slavs" and considered us almost as "low" as Jews. Instead of shooting us, they slowly starved us, confiscating our food and giving it to the Aryans. Even at the Huber farm, I'd seen sacks of grain from Ukraine that I never got to eat.

Did I feel sorry for Sophie? I'm ashamed to say I didn't. She'd finally had a taste of her own medicine.

"Why did you leave?" I asked.

"My Jugend leader came looking for me," she said. "She was starting up a group of guerrilla fighters in the hopes of returning the Nazis to power."

"The Werewolf movement?" I asked.

We'd heard whispers of this group when we were on the road, fleeing the war zone. More than once, an impossibly young boy or girl dressed in oversize Nazi fatigues would jump out of nowhere and start shooting at us. We heard that they'd been instructed to fight to the death.

"I didn't want to join, but she told me she'd execute my family if I refused."

"So you joined?" I pressed her.

"Certain operatives were going undercover, pretending to be refugees but then killing Allied soldiers when they got the chance. I told her I would do it. That's why I was traveling on Bianka's papers and wearing civilian clothing. I blended myself in to a group of refugees, but instead of becoming a Werewolf, I became a refugee. If I go home now, my Jugend leader will kill my family."

Did I believe Sophie? Maybe she was still a Hitler Girl and a Werewolf too. Maybe if she hadn't been caught by the Soviets, she'd be killing Allied soldiers right now.

"How do we know you've truly changed?" I asked.

Sophie stayed silent for a long moment. Then she said, "I saw things when I was stationed with the Jugends in Czechoslovakia . . ."

"Like what?" I asked.

"Things the Nazi soldiers were doing to civilians," she

said. "Even to children." She took a deep, ragged breath and let it out slowly. "I saw the blood. The burial pits. I smelled the burial pits. It confused me. I thought I had been working so we could have a good society."

"But even before you left for Czechoslovakia, you witnessed things the Nazis did," I told her.

Sophie nodded slowly. "But I thought the people being punished were bad. I thought you deserved the treatment I gave you." She squeezed my hand. "I'm sorry, but I really did think that."

Anger boiled inside me, but I tried not to let that show. "Go on," I said.

"The first time I saw an American soldier, I was terrified. I knew what Nazi soldiers did, and I had been taught that the Americans were brutes."

"And what did that first American soldier do?" I asked.

"He gave me a chocolate bar," said Sophie, tears spilling down her face.

"Were you in uniform?" I asked.

"No," she said. "As far as he knew, I was a refugee. But the whole time I was traveling undercover I saw nothing but kindness from British, American, and Canadian soldiers. Even some of the Soviet soldiers were kind. That shocked me."

Sophie's words gave me much to think about, but did

I believe her? I wasn't quite sure. I did believe that she saw Allied soldiers being kind, and that she had wanted to help her family. But I had been the recipient of her cruelty for far too long to think that she could revise her beliefs that quickly.

Elias had woken up and so had Finn. I didn't know how much of our conversation they'd heard, but Elias looked worried. He came over to our side of the room and crouched down. He motioned for the three of us to gather close to him.

"This is no place to talk about what you did during or after the war," he whispered.

"Why?" I asked.

He pointed up. On the ceiling was an unobtrusive round vent. "They could be listening through that," he said. "And the cold in here, the light staying on, the window blocked? That's soft torture."

His words surprised me, but I didn't have time to think about them because just then the door opened. It was the woman with the embroidered blouse, whom the cook had called Galina. She flipped through some pages on a clipboard, then gazed at us one by one. "Bianka Holata?"

Sophie stood up.

"You'll be coming with me."

Galina handcuffed Sophie, and they left.

CHAPTER ELEVEN–
A BATTERED CHAIR
KRYSTIA

Thank goodness it was Sophie they took and not my sister! I scooted closer to Maria and put my arm around her shoulders. I could not bear the thought of being separated from her again, but I had no idea how I could keep us together, and safe.

We all sat in silence, stewing in our own thoughts. What was happening to Sophie right now? I listened carefully to the sounds outside our room and could hear footsteps going deep into the house. I heard the squeak of a door opening and then other metallic sounds from somewhere below. Had they taken Sophie to a cellar?

But I hardly had time to think things through when the door opened again. Instead of the woman, a man in uniform stood there with an unsettling smirk on his face.

He was close enough that I could see the letters *NKVD* emblazoned on his collar tabs. The NKVD was the Soviet equivalent of the Nazi Gestapo: the killers, the interrogators. I felt like throwing up.

"Elias Reisender," he said.

Elias stood up shakily and walked to the door. "I am Elias Reisender," he said.

"You can't separate us," said Finn, jumping to his feet.

"Sit down, son," said Elias, grasping Finn's elbow.

"Believe me," said the NKVD officer to Finn. "It will be better for you if you stay here."

Elias stepped out of the room with the officer, and Finn tried to step out too, but the officer pushed him back in. Finn stumbled and fell, banging his hands on the floor. The NKVD officer slammed the door, and it locked with a firm click.

Finn pounded on the door. Maria stood up and put a hand on Finn's shoulder. "Listen," she said, putting a finger to her lips.

Finn stood still, and we all listened intently. The sounds for Elias were not the same as they had been for Sophie. Faintly, through the walls, we could hear a muffled conversation just beyond our room. My guess was that the NKVD officer was speaking to the soldiers standing guard at the entrance to the mansion. After that, we heard footsteps, and then nothing more.

Was Elias free, or was he being taken to his death? Was it better to go to the basement or out the door? I guessed we'd each find out all too soon.

We were down to three: just Maria, me, and Finn. We sat huddled together from fear, but also to keep warm. I desperately wanted to pee, but I was wearing trousers and couldn't possibly pee in front of Finn.

Hours passed, and each of us drifted in and out of an uneasy sleep. And now that we realized they could be listening, the terrifying monotony was not broken up with conversation.

As we sat there in silence, I thought of what Tato had said about strengths and prejudice. I had managed to trick the Nazis because I used their prejudices to my benefit. But what about these Soviets? Could I do the same with them?

We had lived under Soviet occupation for two years before the Nazis invaded, so I knew a bit about their prejudices. For one, they didn't believe that Ukraine had a unique culture or country but that it was just part of Russia, so to say you were Ukrainian meant you were a traitor. They also thought anyone who didn't believe in Communism was a Nazi, which was kind of strange. From all I had experienced, Communism and Nazism were similar, and the opposite of both was democracy, where all people were equal.

In Soviet eyes, I was probably guilty no matter what I did, by the mere fact that I hadn't died under Nazi occupation. But when they came to our barrack in the American camp, they didn't take everyone. They were selective. And then when we entered the Soviet zone, they identified us as "criminals." Why would that be? All of a sudden, reality came crashing down. They were looking for people who were potential future enemies, which was why nearly all of us were young people.

Sophie was a Werewolf—a possible future threat. Maybe they thought Finn was a Werewolf too.

As for me and Maria, we had both worked with the Ukrainian Insurgent Army, which both the Nazis and the Soviets hated. Was the Ukrainian Insurgent Army seen as a future threat as well? And if they considered it a threat, did they know that we had worked with them?

I was sure Maria and I would be questioned separately, so how would we ever keep our stories straight? How much did they already know about our local network within the Ukrainian Insurgent Army? They would surely compare our statements, looking for inconsistencies. If we spoke about the Underground at all, it would be so easy to let things slip. But how could we not talk about the Underground? Fighting for equality was so much a part of everything that we did.

How could Maria and I get our stories straight if we couldn't talk it through now? The Soviets might be listening through the vent above our cell.

Maria had fallen asleep, so I shook her shoulder gently. She groaned, and her eyes finally fluttered open.

"What is it?" she asked.

I pointed up to the vent so she'd know I was choosing my words carefully. "What do you think the Soviets will ask us when it's our turn to be questioned?"

"They'll just want to know what we did during the war," said Maria, enunciating each word slowly as if she was thinking about it too.

"That's simple enough," I said. "I did housework and cleaning so Mama and I could buy enough food, so we wouldn't starve."

"That's right," said Maria, looking up at the vent. "And I signed up for agricultural work in the Reich because then Mama would have only two mouths to feed instead of three. I wanted to send money back home to help you and Mama out. I had no idea the Nazis weren't going to pay me."

"You and Bohdan Sawchuk signed up together, didn't you?"

"Yes," said Maria. "Bohdan is now in Switzerland."

"And I cleaned houses and did odd jobs during the war," I said. "Nothing too exciting. Toward the end of the war, I was sent for farm work to the Reich, just like you."

"Nothing too exciting," said Maria, nodding her head in agreement.

Those last words were barely out of Maria's mouth when the door opened again. It was Galina.

"Krystia Fediuk?" she said.

I stood up.

"You'll be coming with me."

I bent down, pretending to adjust my shoe and whispered into Maria's ear, "Our stories are simple, and we need to stick to them—even if it kills us."

Maria kissed her fingertips and pressed them to my cheek. "I love you," she said.

Galina snapped one handcuff onto my wrist and the other onto her own. She was silent as she escorted me out of the room and locked the door behind us. I could feel my heart pounding wildly, but I tried to calm myself by breathing slowly. Would she take me out the front door and let me go? Or maybe she'd take me out the front door and order the guards to shoot me. What happened to the people in the basement?

As she tugged me through the reception area, I wanted

to take note of as many things as I could. You never knew what information could be useful. One thing I noticed right away was that Galina was still alone. All the desks were empty. Where had that NKVD man gone? The next thing I noticed was sunlight shining through the window. Daylight, yes, but was it morning or afternoon? I had no idea how much time had passed in that holding cell.

Galina took me down a brightly lit corridor, through an empty kitchen, and toward a metal door. So I was going to the basement.

In order to calm my imagination, I stared at the back of her embroidered blouse, noticing the fine red cross-stitch work on the homespun white linen. The blouse hung loosely from her shoulders as if it were meant for a larger woman, or maybe it had fit her when food was more available. But I also noticed tufts of black fur stuck to the white linen. Did she own a dog?

All dogs used to terrify me. In Ukraine, dogs weren't kept as pets, and some dogs ran wild in the countryside, where they'd attack people from time to time. But Maria had loved Max, the Hubers' farm dog, and even I got to know him. He was as gentle as could be and loved to lick Maria's face. He even licked my face and gave me a lopsided smile with his tongue hanging out. I knew for a fact that if it hadn't been for Max, Maria would have been very lonely on the Huber farm, especially after Bianka escaped. When I found Maria, I think she would have liked to take Max with us when we left, but he was needed by Frau Huber for protection.

If Galina had a friendly dog like Max, maybe she was friendly too. She hadn't been mean to us yet—she'd turned on the light for us and had arranged for us to have food. Maybe there was nothing to be frightened of.

Galina unbolted the metal door, and a dimly lit wooden staircase yawned downward before us: the basement.

"No funny stuff," she said in Russian. "We walk down together."

Did she think I was going to push her down the stairwell? Maybe Sophie would do that sort of thing, or even Maria for that matter, but I couldn't see how that could possibly help me. I wanted Galina to like me, to think of me as human, and then maybe she'd let me go out the front door instead. Then I'd just have to think of a way of getting Maria and the others free.

"Do you have a pet dog?" I asked her.

She looked at me, and her forehead wrinkled. "Why would you ask me such a thing?"

"There's fur on the back of your blouse."

The corners of her lips curved upward slightly, but her response was, "Shut up."

This was not encouraging. I banished the thought of fluffy black dogs from my mind.

My nose wrinkled at a familiar stench. Metallic and sickly sweet. It was a smell that anyone who has lived through war knew well—the thick stink of old blood.

The basement stairs descended into an open area with concrete block walls and no windows. There were two chairs facing each other in the middle of the open area. One was battered and wooden; the smell of blood was the strongest near it. As my eyes adjusted to the light, I saw spatters of blood on the concrete floor; the worn chair had frayed rope knotted on its legs.

I heaved with fear and my knees weakened, but Galina held me up. Had Sophie been tied to this very same chair? Where was she now, and what had she told them?

The woman grabbed a key from a nail on the wall and guided me past the chair and down a corridor to the left. Along the right side of the corridor was a wall of concrete block just like in the open area. Along the left was a row of five rusty metal doors, each one with a small barred window. Jail cells. And they looked like they had been here for a long while. The Soviets couldn't have been the first ones to use this mansion as some sort of prison.

As we passed the first door, a pair of dirt-encrusted hands reached through the bars, and the face of a disheveled teen boy looked out at me. Galina tugged me past him before I could even say a word. The next cell door was open and there was no one inside, but we kept on walking. She stopped me in front of the third cell.

"Why are you putting me in here?" I asked her. "I haven't done anything wrong."

She shoved me into the cell and shut the door in my face. I peered out the barred window and watched her until she was out of view. I heard her boots clomp up the staircase. When she got to the top, she slammed the door shut.

"Let me out," I screamed, pounding on the door.

"It won't do you any good to scream," said a voice from the direction of the first cell. "You may as well save your strength."

"How long have you been here?" I asked the boy.

"Hard to know," he said. "I've lost track of time. I think I've been here for three days, but it could be a week."

A week? I rested my head against the door. What would they do to me? And what would happen to Maria? Would I ever see my sister again?

What would Tato do in this situation? One thing was certain: He wouldn't panic.

I took a deep breath.

I turned and looked at my prison cell.

The damp tile floor looked none too clean, so I was grateful for Olga's shoes. A bare metal cot was bolted to a cement-block wall; the fact that there was no mattress was a good thing because it would have been lice infested for sure. There was a dry, seatless toilet in one of the corners, and the sight of it made me smile. I would be able to pee in the privacy of my own cell instead of embarrassing myself in front of Finn.

Like the room upstairs, there was no window, but the cement-block walls stopped about a hand's width short of the ceiling, so at least there was some ventilation. The air was as chilly as the holding room upstairs, and there was just a single light bulb that cast strange shadows over the narrow cot, the toilet, and the walls. I'd never know how much time had passed or when it was day or night. I stood up and stretched out my arms. I could nearly touch both walls. I wondered if being locked in a place like this was more of what Elias called soft torture?

Was Sophie down here somewhere? Or had she been taken to a different section of this prison house?

"Sophie?" I said in a loud whisper.

"Is that Maria or Krystia?" answered Sophie, her voice sounding ragged and tired.

"Krystia," I said.

"What's happening upstairs?" she asked.

"The NKVD has taken Elias somewhere," I told her.
She didn't answer.

"What about you?" I asked.

"Nothing," she said. "Galina put me in the cell and hasn't been back except to bring you down here."

"What if they're listening?" said the boy from the first cell. "It's better not to talk."

I was about to tell him we weren't talking about anything secret, but then I realized that I had used Sophie's real name instead of calling her Bianka. Maybe I'd given away other information too—things that I didn't even realize.

I stopped talking.

I sat and waited. I got up and paced the room, then sat down again. I lay on the bare cot and closed my eyes, but sleep was the furthest thing from my mind.

A sudden scrape of the door from the top of the stairs. Footsteps that sounded heavier than Galina's. I jumped off the cot and clutched the bars in the window, peering out to the corridor to see what was going on. A man I had never seen before set down a bucket of water and stepped into the corridor. He was wearing army trousers and boots, but instead of a jacket, he wore just an undershirt. He walked down the corridor but didn't pause as he passed the cell with the boy in it. When he got to my cell, he looked right at me. He was so close that I could see the tiny veins in the whites of his eye. I also noticed small red dots on his white undershirt.

Was that blood?

He walked past my cell and continued down the corridor toward Sophie. I shoved my face against the bars and tried to watch, but I was at the wrong angle. I could hear what sounded like a key turning in a lock and a metal door screeching open.

"No," shouted Sophie. "Leave me alone . . ."

I heard grunts and struggling, then suddenly they came into view. The man in the undershirt had Sophie in a tight grip around her waist, but she was trying to pull away. He dragged her past my cell and she was so close that if I reached my fingers out, I could have touched her hair.

Now there were scraping sounds coming from the open area at the base of the stairs. Was he tying Sophie to the chair?

I heard papers rustling. "What is your real name?" asked a man's voice.

"Bianka Holata," answered Sophie. "I'm from Warsaw and I've been working at a farm in Austria for three years."

"The Huber farm near Thaur, correct?" asked the man.

"Yes," said Sophie.

"And yet your fellow captives call you Sophie," he said.

My heart sank. He had been listening. I had gotten Sophie into trouble.

"They, they don't know me," stumbled Sophie. "I think they've mistaken me for someone else."

"And yet you've answered to this name many times since you've come here."

"It's . . . ah . . . my middle name," said Sophie. "I'm Bianka Sophia Holata."

There was a loud slap. Sophie gasped, then whimpered.

"Tell me the truth," said the man.

"But I am telling—"

He slapped again.

Sophie sobbed.

"You are Sophie Huber, are you not?" said the man.

"No," said Sophie. "It's a mistake."

"You're Sophie Huber," said the man. A paper rustled. "I have the report right here. You were in the League of German Girls."

"No," said Sophie. "My name is Bianka Sophia Holata. I was a slave laborer at the Huber farm. I'm from Warsaw."

"You realize that Warsaw is under Soviet control now, don't you?"

Sophie was silent.

"So even if you were Bianka Holata from Warsaw, you'd be rightfully Soviet anyway?"

Sophie said nothing.

"Maybe you'll feel like talking if I clean you up a bit," he said.

"Please . . . *Don't!*" Sophie shouted. I peered out my cell bars and saw rivulets of water coursing down the hallway.

"I'm s-s-sooo c-c-cold . . . ," said Sophie.

The man went back up the stairs.

Sophie sobbed. And even though I despised her, I felt sorry for her. I was freezing too, and I hadn't just been doused with water.

If I had been fed Nazi propaganda the way she was, would I have turned out the same as her? It was hard to know. But right now, I desperately wanted to go out there and comfort her.

I sat on my cot and held my head in my hands and wept. What was to become of us all? Already, Piotr and Olga were dead, Elias had been taken by the NKVD, and Sophie was being interrogated. What was happening to Maria? Was she still in the cell with Finn, or had she been moved somewhere else too? The thought of losing her again terrified me.

I tried to think of all the good things, like Auntie Stefa and Canada, but it didn't work. I wasn't even sure my aunt would remember us. And even if she did, maybe she didn't want two starving and broken nieces to come and live with her. I wrapped my arms around my knees and rocked myself back and forth. I thought back to the time when our family was whole, before Tato died of lung cancer and before Mama was hanged for hiding Jews.

The image of Tato on his deathbed came back to me. I could almost feel the warmth of his grip as he held my hand that one last time. "You are my eldest daughter, Krystia," he'd said. "And I am grateful for your strength."

What strength did I have now? I took a deep breath, then let it out slowly.

I had now listened to an interrogation. It was no longer an unknown fear. I had to make my mind strong enough to get through my own questioning. I had to make them think I was nothing but a simple girl.

I could do that.

I held my hand to my heart and said under my breath, "Tato, please give me and Maria the strength that we need to get through this. Please give Sophie the strength too." I curled up on my cot and drifted into an uneasy sleep, thinking of Sophie, cold, shivering, and wet.

Untold hours later, I woke with a jolt. The door upstairs squeaked open, and lighter footsteps sounded on the stairs.

"Here," said a woman. It sounded like Galina.

"Thank you," said Sophie, her voice chattering. "I am so c-c-cold."

"It would be better if you confessed," said Galina.

"We know that you're Sophie Huber. Your description was sent to us."

"But I'm not—"

"Stop this instant," said Galina in a firm voice. "Your name is on our list of suspected Werewolf operatives. Those who have been apprehended and were carrying weapons have been executed. You had no weapons. They should treat you more leniently, but only if you stop this ridiculous denial of who you are."

Sophie gasped for breath, and I heard her weeping. Finally, she said, "I confess. I am Sophie Huber, and I was in the Jugend. I was approached by a Werewolf leader and ordered to join, so I did."

"Who was your Werewolf leader?" asked Galina.

Sophie was silent.

"You need to answer me," said the woman.

Sophie whimpered, then took in a deep and ragged breath. "Gruppenführerin Eloise Winter of Innsbruck," she finally said.

"Who else did she recruit in addition to yourself?"

Silence.

"Sophie, this is information you need to tell me if you want to avoid execution."

"But Gruppenführerin Winter ordered our entire Hitler Youth group to join the Werewolves."

"Here's the membership list of your Jugend group," said the woman. "I will read the names out one at a time. If you say nothing, I will assume that person is a Werewolf member."

Sophie wept and sniffled.

Galina read out girls' names one by one, pausing after each name, but Sophie didn't speak. She didn't stand up for a single one of her friends.

"It should go well for you. We can add these girls to our list of criminals. Now, tell me, what did you do as a Werewolf?"

"I didn't do anything."

"What do you mean?"

"I was instructed to blend in with refugees fleeing the battle zone," said Sophie. "I guess I did do that, but she wanted me to kill Allied military personnel, and I never did that. I have no weapons and never intended to carry out her orders."

Galina was silent. Sophie continued.

"I just wanted to get away. To survive."

"I will have your confession typed up," said the woman. "Once you sign it, you will leave this basement."

I peered out through the bars, hoping to get a glimpse of what was going on. Sophie passed by my cell, wrapped in a blanket, with her damp hair hanging in coils over her face. Galina had her arm around Sophie's waist, and she was leading her back to her cell.

I heard the rusty squeak of the cell door at the end of the corridor opening again, then it was closed with a loud slam and a screech of the key in the lock.

Galina paused in front of my cell. "You will be interrogated next," she said.

CHAPTER TWELVE– KEEPING WARM
MARIA

I tried to stay strong as I watched my sister being escorted out of our holding cell by Galina. I even tried to take comfort in the fact that she'd been taken by Galina and not that man in the NKVD uniform. That had to be a good sign, didn't it?

But then it made me worry about Elias. I looked over at Finn. He held his head in his hands, and I could see a tear plop onto the ground. The NKVD were executioners. I hated to think about what was happening to Elias right now.

"We'll get out of this somehow," I said to Finn, patting his shoulder.

He raised his head and glared at me with his tear-filled eyes. "Enough with the lying. We're going to die in here, and you know it."

I opened my mouth to argue but remembered that

someone could be listening, so instead I just glared back at him and squeezed his hand. He opened his mouth to say something else, but I put my finger to my lips, then pointed to the ceiling. Finn sighed.

"We need to keep warm," he said.

Finn and I had been prisoners together for more than a day in the truck, so he was no longer a stranger, but could I call him my friend? The thought of wrapping my arms around a boy I hardly knew made my face feel hot with embarrassment. But even more embarrassing than that was the fact that I desperately had to pee.

"I agree that we'll need to share body heat somehow," I said in as dignified a tone as I could muster. "But before we figure that out, can you do me a big favor?"

"Ah . . . sure," said Finn.

"Stand in that corner and face the wall," I said.

He looked confused for a moment, and then his eyes widened. "Oh, right," he said. His face turned bright pink. "I'll stand in the corner."

I went over to the toilet and tried to pee, but even though I was bursting, nothing happened.

"What's the matter?" asked Finn, his face resolutely turned away from me.

"I don't know," I said. "It's like my bladder is too shy to pee in front of you."

"I have a solution," he said. "I'll sing a song. Then you'll have complete privacy."

He clasped his hands behind his back and faced the wall. He sang the first lines of an old German folk song called "Die Gedanken Sind Frei"—"Thoughts Are Free." It was a song that irritated the Nazis. I figured it might also irritate the Soviets, but I loved this song. I hummed along as my bladder relaxed:

Thoughts are free, no one can guess them
Like shadows they flee, nobody can catch them
No stranger can find them, no hunter can shoot them
So it always shall be: Thoughts are free!

I groaned with relief as I peed out what felt like entire buckets, then as I pulled up my underwear, I turned around to push the handle and remembered that it didn't work! The bowl was filled with my very concentrated stinky pee, and now the two of us would be subjected to its smell in this stuffy room that didn't even have a usable window. I could feel my face getting hot with embarrassment, and I was sure that it was now as red as Finn's.

"I'm all done, Finn," I said. "You can turn around."

"Now you can sing the second verse to the wall," he said. "I need to use the toilet too."

"Oh!" I said. "Are you sure you have to go right now?" I was mortified by the thought of Finn seeing how much I had peed. Worse yet, I had no way of washing my hands. I wiped them on my skirt, more for show than anything else.

"I do have to go right now," said Finn, his cheeks bright red. "Please just turn the other way and sing."

What could I do? I would just have to live with the embarrassment. With everything else we had been through together I tried to convince myself that this was nothing to worry about.

I gave Finn a brave smile as we passed each other in the cell, and then I faced the wall. Even though I liked Finn's song, I didn't want to sing another verse of it. Instead, I sang a Ukrainian folk song from when I was a kid, "Hrechanyky," about buckwheat pancakes. Maybe our Russian soldiers knew it as well:

Mother went to the village
To get buckwheat flour,
To make buckwheat pancakes
To feed her babies.
Hop, my pancakes
Hop, my white ones,
I don't know why

My pancakes won't rise.
Hop, my pancakes
Hop, my delicious ones,
I don't know why
My pancakes aren't good.

Singing that song took my mind off the sound of Finn at the toilet, but it also made me hungry. How I would love to have a plate of thin buckwheat pancakes stuffed with cheese . . .

Suddenly the toilet gurgled.

I stopped singing. "Did it flush itself?" I asked.

"Yes," said Finn. "Come and look!"

I ran over to look; sure enough it was empty. "That toilet is the strangest thing I've ever seen," I said, and I couldn't help but giggle.

The whole incident with the self-flushing toilet and singing those songs had put me in a better frame of mind. And, of course, it also helped that I didn't feel like I was about to burst. There was still the matter of keeping warm, but I was starting to feel less self-conscious about being alone with Finn.

I sat down on the ground and patted the spot beside me. Finn slid down close beside me. In a voice I could barely hear, he said, "By sitting this close, we can whisper."

In a louder voice, he said, "Your hands are blue. Let me warm them up in mine."

My hands felt like solid blocks of ice, but I had tried to ignore the discomfort. I slipped my hands inside Finn's, and gradually they began to warm up. "Thank you," I said.

I turned my head so that my mouth was close to his ear and said in a low whisper, "We need to get out of here, and we need to be careful of what we say if we're interrogated."

Finn nodded. He turned his mouth to my ear and whispered, "We should take turns sleeping. We need to stay alert."

"You sleep first," I said.

Finn draped his jacket over his shoulders and curled into a tight ball on the floor. I stayed sitting with my arms wrapped around my knees and stared at the light bulb, but though my hands were warmed, I could not stop shivering. I looked at Finn—his teeth were chattering.

This was so awkward. We needed to share our body warmth or we would both freeze. What would Mama say about this situation? And I thought about her words: *Break your problems into smaller pieces.*

Our current problem was the cold. I didn't know Finn well enough to call him my friend, but he and his father had been kind and respectful. And we were prisoners together with a common goal—to escape.

Could I cuddle him? If it meant helping us both stay alive, the answer was yes.

I lay down behind Finn and wrapped my arm around his chest, then grabbed his hands in mine again. As I lay there, warming Finn and warming myself, I thought of Krystia. What was happening to her? Was she still alive? Was she still in this building? By the sound of it, she was likely in the basement with Sophie. What about Elias? I could only hope and pray that we'd all survive somehow.

Hours passed, but with the never-changing light bulb and the window blocked, it was impossible to know if it was day or night. I stayed awake by sheer willpower as I felt Finn's shivering gradually subside. But as Finn's warmth enveloped me, my ability to stay awake fled. I fell into a deep and dreamless sleep.

CHAPTER THIRTEEN– "SHCHEDRYK"

KRYSTIA

I watched through the bars in my door as Galina came down the stairs again, lugging a pail. If she was going to douse me with icy water, at least I'd be prepared. Cold water wouldn't make me talk. I hoped there was nothing she could do to me that would make me talk.

But I was unnerved by the questions that Sophie had been asked. The interrogator didn't care that she was a vile, hateful, and devoted Nazi all through the war. All she was interested in was collecting names of Sophie's Werewolf group. It seemed the Soviets wanted to punish people in advance for possible future crimes and were ignoring the crimes of the past.

This meant all my clearly anti-Nazi actions would be of no interest to my interrogator. All she wanted would be names from my group—the unit of the Ukrainian Insurgent Army that operated near Viteretz. Our resistance movement fought the Nazis during the war, but Galina wouldn't care about that. Now that the Nazis were defeated, my interrogator would know that Ukraine's biggest threat came from the Soviets. She would want to cut the freedom movement off at its knees. Would she hunt down and kill Uncle Ivan, Auntie Iryna, our network of friends? Thank goodness neither my sister nor I had been in touch with anyone back home for several months. Our information wasn't current. But what if I gave her something useful by mistake?

I could hear Galina set the pail down in front of the first cell, then the sound of something being dipped into the pail. A clink of the bars and Galina said to the boy, "Here's some water."

Drinking water, not torture! I licked my own parched lips in anticipation. The boy gulped it down loudly.

"More, please," he said.

"That's enough," she answered.

He sighed deeply in response, and I could feel his thirst. My tongue felt like sandpaper.

She lugged the pail farther down the corridor and stopped in front of my cell. She dipped in a metal cup and passed it through the bars in my window. I looked in the cup, expecting it to be water, but it looked more like a weak tea.

"Drink," she said. "I don't have all day."

I took a sip. It tasted like water that dirty potatoes had been washed in. There was another taste too: something bitter. But it was wet, and it soothed my dry lips and tongue and throat. She reached in for the cup before I was half-finished, so I gulped the rest down quickly and handed the empty cup back to her.

I tried to hold the final mouthful of wetness on my tongue, to relish it and make it last, but almost against my will I swallowed it, and soon my mouth was nearly as parched as before.

Once Sophie downed her tin of murky water in her cell, the woman went back upstairs. The door slammed, and we were left in an uneasy silence.

I knew that I was about to be tortured—or as Galina called it, "interrogated"—and knowing that it was about to happen was in itself a form of torture. Every time there was a sound upstairs my heart quickened at the thought of being tied to that chair, of being confronted by either Galina or that man in the blood-spattered shirt.

I paced back and forth in my little cell, then sat on the cot, but I couldn't keep still. I was desperate to find out more about that boy locked up in the first cell. The more I knew from him, the better I could prepare myself. And strange as it may have been, I also wanted to give comfort to Sophie. We were definitely not friends, but we were fellow prisoners, and I hated that they'd hurt her.

But how could I communicate with my fellow captives without giving our captors information to use against us? I looked up to the ceiling and tried to figure out where there was an opening or a microphone that they could listen through. As far as I could tell, there were no openings. But from Sophie's interrogation, it really did sound like they'd been listening to us. So how could I give comfort to my fellow prisoners and perhaps also get information from them without the soldiers upstairs hearing our conversations?

All at once, it came to me: We could sing. I'd have to choose carefully because so many of the songs I knew would make our Soviet captors angry. I couldn't sing a hymn because they hated religion. I couldn't sing a lot of the Ukrainian traditional songs because so many of them were about being captured and imprisoned by the Russians. Maybe Sophie knew a song or two from before the war? Maybe that boy did too. Singing would be a way to pass the time and get our minds off our situation.

In a very low voice, I began to sing the "Shchedryk"—a

very old Ukrainian folk song—so old that it dated back to the time before Christ. I figured that since it was pre-Christian, the Soviets shouldn't hate it. It was also one that people from all over the world recognized and could be sung in many languages and with different lyrics. Before the war, we would go door-to-door on Christmas Eve, singing it to our neighbors, even though it had nothing to do with Christmas. At the beginning of the war, when the Soviets occupied our town, we were forbidden to sing hymns, but we got away with singing the "Shchedryk."

As I sang the "Shchedryk," the boy in the first cell joined in. His voice was ragged and weak when he started, but the singing gave him strength. His words were slightly different from mine, but the tune was the same. As we reached the last line of the last verse, the boy started up again, but this time he sang the exact same words as me. This was a much better way to pass the time than worrying about my upcoming torture session.

We had sung it half a dozen times when Sophie said, "That melody is so familiar, but what do the words mean?"

I couldn't tell her that the meaning transcended the words. The meaning was for hope and freedom from oppression. The words were simpler, so I told her those.

"It's about a little swallow flying in through the

window," I said. "Getting us to notice all the good things, like the baby sheep and lambs that have just been born, the grain growing in the fields, all that we have to look forward to."

"I remember that melody from when I was little," said Sophie. "But it was about bells ringing. That was way before the war."

"Do you remember the words?" I asked.

"No," she said. "But please sing it again if you like. I can hum along. It's so beautiful."

As we sang, the boy changed a word here and there. At first I thought he'd forgotten the lyrics, but then I realized he was trying to tell us something in a way that maybe the eavesdroppers wouldn't understand. It was just a different word every verse or two, but I pieced it together.

His name was Mychailo, and he was from Belarus. He was only sixteen! He looked older but I guess he had aged from being tortured and imprisoned. From the sound of it, his village was close to the Polish border. Of his entire family, he and his grandmother were the only ones who survived the war.

We sang for hours, and I only stopped because my voice became too hoarse to continue. I had no idea if it was day or night, but I was so exhausted that I lay down on the bare metal cot and fell into a deep sleep.

*　　*　　*

I woke with a jolt. How much time had passed? Was it time for my torture? I gulped for breath, and my body shook uncontrollably. The walls seemed to close in on me. I curled up in a ball, frozen with fear.

But then I heard the lyrics of "Shchedryk" in my mind, and I remembered how happy I used to be when Tato was still alive. Our whole family would go out caroling together.

Even here in this awful place, singing that song with Mychailo and Sophie had brought some peace. My voice was still too hoarse to sing, so I thought about the lyrics and sang the song in my head—and in my head Tato sang along. How I wished Tato were here with me now, to protect me and to keep me company. I closed my eyes and his image appeared in my imagination.

What is your strength in this situation? he'd asked.

Those words made my heart ache. Tato always thought I was strong, even when he lay dying.

I opened my eyes and got up off the cot. I stretched and took in a deep breath, then slowly let it out again. I paced slowly from one end of my tiny cell to the other, then turned and did it over again. As I paced, I listed out things that made me strong:

Maria was alive, as far as I knew, and she was just one floor away from me.

The lice powder the Americans sprayed us with at their camp was still working.

Olga's shoes protected my feet.

I had a toilet and the privacy to use it.

I recently had had something to drink.

I had light.

I had listened to an interrogation, so I was a little bit prepared for my own.

I kept on pacing until my heartbeat settled down and my shoulders relaxed. I took in a deep breath, grateful for my strengths.

CHAPTER FOURTEEN–
A LENGTH OF ROPE
MARIA

The sound of the door opening jolted me out of a deep and dreamless sleep. Galina stood in our holding room, hands on hips and a smirk on her face.

"I see you've gotten friendly," she said.

I sat up quickly and pushed Finn away in embarrassment. That movement shocked Finn awake. He rubbed his eyes, then all at once seemed to realize where he was.

I got to my feet and faced her.

"I need to see my sister."

"Shut up," she said.

She handcuffed Finn and me together and led us to the office area at the front of the mansion. That room had windows, but outside it was dark. Was it the middle of the night? I was so confused about night and day.

When we had first arrived, the only person in the office had been Galina, but now the other three desks were occupied. Standing in front of the empty desk was the kerchiefed woman who had brought in our soup. She waited now with her hands clasped and an anxious look on her lined face. At the desk across from her sat a scary-looking man in a blood-spattered white undershirt. He was filling out a form on the typewriter, pecking away one finger at a time. The NKVD officer who had taken Elias away sat at the desk behind him, and across from him was a woman NKVD officer. Those two were in a deep discussion, but they stopped talking as Finn and I walked through.

Galina led us down a brightly lit corridor and into a kitchen area that had been stripped down to the essentials. Whoever had lived here before the war had left no lasting imprint. The floral textured wallpaper had been painted over in a dull institutional gray, and the stone-tiled floor was cracked and heaving. A scratched kitchen table that looked as if it had been brought in from somewhere else was surrounded by an odd assortment of chairs. There was a basket of potatoes on the counter, as well as a bag of onions, and a battered pot on the stove.

And then I saw the metal door. Was that how you got to the cellar? Was Krystia down there? Maybe Sophie too?

Galina opened a drawer and drew out two potato

peelers. Handing one to Finn and one to me, she said, "Wash and peel enough of those potatoes to fill the pot up halfway. Peel the onions and leave them on the counter. And no funny business."

She turned and walked back toward the office.

This seemed almost too good to be true. Was she really leaving us in a room where we had access to food and water, tools (no matter how dull), and maybe even access to Krystia and Sophie?

Finn smiled and was about to say something, but I pointed up to the ceiling, which had vents. Was someone listening? Was this a trap? I held a finger to my lips.

Finn nodded.

Then I pointed to the metal door and pointed to my ear. His eyes widened in understanding: We needed to listen for any sound of Krystia and Sophie, in case that's where they were being held.

For now, we would do exactly what we'd been ordered to do. That, and maybe have a bite of raw potato and a few sips of water . . .

Finn filled the pot about half full with water. Our routine was to peel a potato, wash it under the tap, then put it into the pot of water so it wouldn't turn brown. We hadn't been asked to cook the potatoes, so we left the stove turned off.

Each potato washed was an opportunity to have a sip of

water from the tap and each potato peeled was an opportunity to have a bit of potato to munch on. We worked in silence, our ears tuned to the basement, but I didn't hear a thing.

The kitchen was warmer than our holding cell, and it was good to have something to do instead of sitting and waiting and worrying. And it was nothing short of glorious to have those sips of water and bits of potato peel. I only wished there was some way we could get food and water to Krystia and Sophie—and Elias if he was still alive.

It must have been hours later when the man in the bloodied undershirt stepped into the kitchen. He grunted when he saw what we were doing and wordlessly fished out a clean peeled potato from the pot on the stove.

As he bit into it and chewed, I noticed the length of rope hanging out of his back pocket. The potato peeler slipped out of my hand and clattered onto the floor. The man in the undershirt picked it up and handed it back to me. I took it with shaking hands.

He held out the rest of his potato as if it were an apple. "Tasty," he said, smiling. He popped it into his mouth and swallowed it down, then dried his hands on his trousers and opened the metal door.

Before he closed it, I caught the stench of old blood and a glimpse of steps going downward. My knees buckled. I clutched the side of the counter to keep from falling. Finn grabbed my arm to steady me, and I took a deep breath. Was Krystia down there? What would that man do to her?

Within minutes, the metal door opened again. The man in the undershirt smirked as he walked past us, and I noticed that he no longer had that rope in his back pocket.

Galina came into the kitchen moments later. "You two are done here," she said.

CHAPTER FIFTEEN– ROXY
KRYSTIA

The door upstairs creaked. Moments later, a key was shoved into my lock and my door swung open. The man in the bloody undershirt put a meaty hand around my arm. "Your turn to answer some questions," he said.

I tried to pull away, but his grip was firm. He took me out of the cell and down the corridor. As he dragged me past the first cell, Mychailo caught my eye and he nodded. This gave me strength.

I was dragged to the open area at the base of the stairs and shoved down onto the chair. My body shook as the man took a long rope out of his back pocket and tied my hands behind my back. He tied my left ankle to one chair leg and the right ankle to the other. Then for good measure, he looped the rope around my waist, pulling it so tightly that it dug into my hip bones.

Once he finished, I expected him to sit in the chair across from me and begin the interrogation, but he didn't do that. Instead, he went back up the stairs, leaving me alone to stew in my worry. I looked down at the floor around my chair, and my heart quickened at the sight of so many pinpoints of dried blood.

I took a deep breath and let it out slowly.

In my mind, I heard Tato say, *You are my strong daughter.*

I took in another deep breath and slowly exhaled. My heart slowed down.

I thought about Sophie's interrogation.

She was slapped. She was dowsed with cold water.

I could get through that.

The door upstairs opened again, but instead of hearing bootsteps, there was ragged breathing and a shuffling and clacking of something bounding down the stairs. My heart fluttered wildly, wondering what sort of monster this was.

A huge black dog with a wide, slobbery jaw locked his menacing eyes on mine, and I nearly fainted on the spot. For a mere second, the dog paused, but then he lunged at me, nearly knocking my chair sideways.

The dog's powerful front paws ripped through the

sleeve of my blouse, and it growled and grunted as it sniffed my neck and nipped at the cloth tied around the wound on my head. The dog's teeth tugged on the bandage until it loosened and fell to the ground. I felt his cold nose first, sniffing wetly at my wound, and then his warm tongue licked it. I wanted to cringe, to push the dog away, and I stifled a scream. I thought of those wild dogs back home that could tear a person apart in an instant.

All at once I had a flash of memory. Tato feeding a honeybee Mama's berry jam at our kitchen table. Tato didn't get stung. *A honeybee can smell fear,* said Tato. *They attack when they smell fear.*

Did dogs smell fear?

I would not allow myself to smell of fear. I thought of Max, the beautiful dog at the Huber farm who befriended Maria. Max was my friend too, for the short time I was there. Max also loved to lick and nuzzle just like this scary black dog was doing.

I forced myself to close my eyes in case the dog might see my open eyes as a threat. I let my muscles go limp and made my heart slow down. I took deep breaths and ignored the cold wet nose that now prodded my armpit.

"Roxy, come here." The woman's voice.

Roxy was a girl's name. A girl dog.

I opened my eyes. Galina sat in the chair across from

me. In one hand she held a clipboard. Her other hand was looped through Roxy's leather collar. The woman's lips were curved into a smile, but her eyes were cold. "I thought you'd like to see my pet dog," she said.

Roxy yipped, and her front paws scrabbled on the floor, but Galina held on to her with a tight grip.

I breathed in slowly, then breathed out, feeling my strength. I met the woman's eyes and smiled back at her. "Roxy is a beautiful dog," I said.

Roxy stopped struggling at the sound of her name.

"Such a beautiful dog, Roxy girl," I said, in the same calming tone I had used with Krasa, our family cow.

Roxy's tail thumped. She cocked her head and looked at me, and if I didn't know better, I'd say she was smiling.

The woman frowned. Her plan to frighten me wasn't working. She let go of Roxy's collar, and the dog bounded back up to me, but I stayed relaxed. Roxy sniffed my shoes, and I forced myself not to flinch at the sensation of her cold wet nose on my ankle.

"Good girl," I said in a melodic voice. "Roxy is such a beautiful girl."

The woman's mouth was a thin, flat line. She stood and walked up the stairs, opening the door at the top. "Roxy," she shouted. "Get up here."

Roxy clattered up the stairs, and Galina slammed the door behind her.

She came back down a minute later and sat heavily in the wooden chair across from me again. She set the clipboard on her lap and flipped a few pages in.

"Now," she said. "What did you do during the war?"

"For most of the war, I stayed in Viteretz with Mama," I told her. "Everyone was required to work. I was mostly assigned to clean houses."

"Who did you live with?"

"Mama," I said.

"And after she was killed, and your house confiscated by the Nazis. Where did you live then?"

I looked her in the eyes and answered slowly, "With the priest's wife for a while, and then with a relative." This was true. I lived with my auntie Iryna in the woods at the encampment for the Ukrainian Insurgent Army, but I wouldn't tell her that.

"Which relative?" she asked.

"Polina Semko," I lied. "A distant cousin."

"But your aunt and uncle were very close by," she said. My heart fluttered with anxiety. "Why didn't you go to live with either Iryna Fediuk or Ivan Pidhirney?"

"Cousin Polina is old," I said. "And she needed my help."

The woman nodded, but her eyebrows were knitted in

thought. She flipped through the papers on her clipboard, and I took in another long slow breath.

"Who dug the hole in your kitchen floor?" she asked.

The question took me by surprise. How did she even know about this?

"What do you mean?" I asked.

She leaned forward and slapped me hard across the face. "The hiding place. Where you hid your Jewish friends. Who dug the hole?"

Uncle Ivan had dug the hole. The ground was hard clay, and Mama and I couldn't do it on our own, but I couldn't tell her that, or she'd know I'd been in contact with the Ukrainian Insurgent Army. "I dug it."

"Impossible," she said.

"Mama helped."

She slapped me on the jaw. "You're not a good liar."

I looked her in the eyes and tried not to blink.

She made a low growl under her breath and flipped through her notes once more. "Your papers have you working at the Huber farm with your sister," she said.

"Yes," I replied, relieved for the change of topic.

"We know what you really did." She held up my work papers. "This forgery might fool the Nazis, but it doesn't fool us."

I was surprised that she realized my papers were

forged. Uncle Ivan's counterfeit documents were the best that the Underground produced. "I was assigned to the Huber farm," I said. "Along with my sister."

"That's the letter of the truth," said Galina. "But you and I both know you only got to the Huber farm near the end of the war."

She was correct. I said nothing in response but just stared at her.

"Your uncle Ivan and aunt Iryna are well-known for their traitorous actions toward the Soviet Union," she said. "And of course, you know that the Ukrainian Insurgent Army is a pro-Nazi group."

My face went hot with anger. "The Ukrainian Insurgent Army is an anti-Nazi group."

As soon as the words were out, I wished that I could have taken them back. I had just admitted to her that I knew all about the Ukrainian Insurgent Army.

Galina smiled at me. "So, you are aware of your aunt and uncle's involvement with that treasonous group," she said.

I stared her down and tried not to react. So much was lost and all because I let my emotions take over. I couldn't let her trick me again. I concentrated on my breathing, slowly taking air into my lungs, then letting it back out again as slowly as I could. I vowed not to give her any more information.

"Your uncle dug the hole beneath your kitchen floor," she said. "You were in constant contact with the underground group, and after your mother was executed for hiding Jews, you lived with those traitors."

Did someone give up this information under torture? Or had there been a Soviet spy in our underground unit? My mind raced at the possibilities for betrayal.

I said nothing.

She flipped through her sheets. "I have a list of the people who are in the same underground unit as your aunt and uncle," she said. "I'll read through the list. If someone is not a member, you need to tell me. If you stay silent, I'll assume they are all members, and therefore traitors to be hunted down and killed."

This was a dilemma. If I said nothing, all the people would be killed, but if I said something, she'd know that I knew who was in that unit, and she'd interrogate me for more information on a wider net of people.

"No," I said. "But I can tell you something else that might be of use to you."

"And what's that?" she asked, leaning forward.

"Their members use code names. Not even one of their soldiers would be able to answer your question reliably."

Galina stood up and slapped me across the face. I felt a spurt of warmth from one nostril, then tasted a gush of salty blood on my lip. My eyes filled with tears, but I glared at her with defiance.

"Do you really think you can fool me?" she asked. "Yes, they use code names, but these are people from your own community. You grew up with them. You know them."

"You can punish me all you want," I said. "But I'm just a simple girl who cleaned houses for a while, and after that I did farmwork in Austria." I closed my eyes, and my head slumped forward.

Galina paced in front of me. "You are traveling on forged documents, which is a punishable offense. You assisted the Ukrainian Insurgent Army, a group traitorous to the Soviet Union. I can order you shot for this."

I raised my head and met her eyes, but I didn't say a word.

"You're just a child, though," she said in a gentler tone. "I can put in a good word for you. Just tell me how to find their encampment."

I didn't reply.

We stared at each other for long minutes, but finally Galina said, "This isn't the end of it."

She left me there, tied to the chair, and she slowly walked back up the steps.

As I sat, powerless, my mind raced, reviewing what I'd said. I was fairly certain that I hadn't given anything away.

And I was proud of myself for not letting her read out that list of names. The only piece of information I gave her, about the code names, was something that everyone knew. I was relieved that she didn't ask any questions about Maria. Maybe Galina didn't know that Maria helped Nathan escape on papers supplied by the Underground. I had to make sure that she never found out.

CHAPTER SIXTEEN-
THE BLUE ROOM
MARIA

Galina grabbed me and Finn each by an elbow and led us to the office area. She looked over to where the NKVD officers were working at their desks. The blinds were closed, so I had no idea if it was morning yet.

"Can one of you deal with this boy?" Galina said. "I'll interview the girl myself."

The woman NKVD officer stood up. "I'll take him," she said, leading Finn to a back room.

I was forced up the battered wooden staircase with Galina close behind me. The stairs curved into a wide semicircle. We passed a landing for the second floor, which revealed a long hallway of closed doors. We kept climbing to the third floor. The staircase opened up into the middle of a circular hallway with four rooms; just like on the floor below, all the doors were closed. Galina opened one of the doors and pushed me in, locking the door behind me.

I practically tripped over the chairs that stood in the middle of the small room. They had been positioned to face each other. From the slanted walls and the blue stained glass window, I knew that this room must be in one of the towers I had seen from the road. The window was made with a wavy kind of glass, which made it difficult to see outside, but some light did shine through, so I figured it might be early morning.

Of all the rooms to be put in, dare I say that I was grateful to be put in one where the sun shone through blue glass? It was like Mama was gazing at me. I reached into my jacket pocket and took out the bit of blue cloth. I held it to my face and breathed in the scent that wasn't Mama's but reminded me of her.

"Please, Mama," I whispered. "Help me break this situation into manageable pieces."

The blue glass helped. Another good thing about this room was that it was warmer than the cell, so I was comfortable. In fact, after sitting for a while, it was even a little bit stuffy, so I took off my jacket and draped it over the back of my chair.

I tried to use the waiting time to my advantage, going

over in my mind the things a questioner might ask, and the topics I had to avoid. Then all too soon the door opened.

Thank goodness it was only Galina.

She walked up and slapped me hard across the face!

"What did you do that for?" I asked, wincing at the pain.

She slapped me across the jaw again, then sat down. She had a scowl on her face.

She pulled my identity papers out of her jacket pocket and threw them onto my lap. "You take a look at them," she said. "And you tell me what doesn't add up."

"But . . . ," I said, flipping through the pages. "They're in order. I worked at the Huber farm in Austria since the fall of 1942."

"But you weren't kidnapped. You voluntarily went to the Reich labor office in Lviv and signed up."

I slid down in my chair. She was right about that. I was one of the first in my area to leave, and I did volunteer. But not because I wanted to help the Nazis; it was to help Nathan. His false documents identified him as Bohdan Sawchuk, and I was terrified that he'd be caught out, so I went with him to help him pass as a Ukrainian. But I couldn't tell her that because his papers had been forged by Uncle Ivan and the Underground.

I held my head in my hands. "I am so ashamed," I told her.

"What is it that you're ashamed of?" she asked.

"Of being so stupid," I said. "I believed the posters that the Nazis put up, saying that they would pay farmworkers from Ukraine, and that I would be able to send the money home to help my family."

"You wanted to help the Nazis?" she asked.

"No! I got a job so I could support my family," I answered.

"You're a traitor," she said. "And you should be shot."

"But I'm not a traitor . . . ," I began to say, then stopped.

Galina looked up, interested. "Go on," she said. "You look like a smart and brave girl. What were you really up to?"

I said nothing. Better for her to think I was stupid than to let her know that I was working with the Underground.

Galina sat there and waited, but I kept my mouth shut. She leaned back and smiled. "I can sit here all day," she said. "You may as well talk."

I sat up straight and felt the edges of the blue cloth in my pocket. I looked into her eyes and said, "Thank you for helping to defeat the Nazis. Please believe that I would never betray my country." I felt good about that line because it wasn't even a lie. My country was Ukraine, not the Soviet Union, and I would never betray it.

"You'll have to do better than that," she said.

I willed my face to look friendly and relaxed. We stared at each other for a long time. It could have even been an hour. When she finally got up, the room was bathed in bright blue from the stained glass window.

She went out the door and locked it behind her.

As the hours passed, the room became stuffy and hot, and I worried about what would happen next. And from the room beside me I could hear slaps and scrapes and screams from the voice of a stranger. How many people were prisoners in this mansion? Did Galina leave my room to question the person beside me, or was it one of the other officers doing that interrogation?

I took the blue cloth out of my pocket and held it to my cheek, and I let the blue light wash over me, as if it were Mama hugging me. I tried to feel calm, but my heart pounded with anxiety. What would happen to me? Where was Krystia? Being left alone with my own imagination was even worse than having Galina staring me down.

And then the door opened.

It wasn't Galina but the man with the blood-spattered undershirt. "Time for your sister to see you," he said, smirking. He fastened my wrists together with handcuffs and led me out the door.

CHAPTER SEVENTEEN-
CONFESSION
KRYSTIA

The rope dug painfully into my hip, and my wrists were raw, but at least with Olga's shoes, my feet weren't as cold as they could have been. I felt suspended in time: There was no day or night but just one long interminable moment. When the door above scraped open again, I could hardly register the fact. It felt like a dream.

When Galina appeared, she had a clipboard in one hand and a pail of water in the other. She set the pail onto the floor about a meter in front of me. I prayed that it was filled with water to drink and not water to torment me with.

A tin cup was hooked onto the side. I licked my dry lips with anticipation. Still holding on to the clipboard, she walked past me as if I didn't exist. I could hear her footsteps go all the way to the end of the corridor and then stop.

"Your confession," Galina said to someone.

"I can't read this," said Sophie. "It's in Russian."

"Just sign it," said Galina.

I heard pen scraping on paper. Sophie must have signed. Galina walked a few more steps.

"Your turn to sign," she said.

Mychailo grunted out a bitter laugh. "You write good fairy tales," he said. "I never admitted to any of this, but I know better than to argue. Pass me the pen and I'll sign it."

"A wise decision."

When she was finally back in front of me, I wondered if she was about to give me a confession too, but how could I read a confession or sign it when I was all tied up? She set her clipboard down and loosened the rope that bound my wrists.

The blood began to flow back into my hands, and the numbness began to leave, but there was also an intense stabbing sensation of a thousand pins and needles. I rubbed my palms together and stretched out my fingers. She shoved a paper into my hands, but my fingers didn't work yet, and the paper fell to the ground.

She slapped me hard with the back of her hand.

"Clumsy girl." She picked the paper back up and set it on my lap.

My hands still tingled, but I did my best to hold the paper and try to read the Russian words. She wanted me to acknowledge that I was a Nazi collaborator! It was such an absurd statement that in other circumstances it might have been funny. I would have signed the document if I was the only one it got into trouble. But the confession identified Auntie Iryna and Uncle Ivan and listed a location that I knew was a safe house. It implicated many people in our town, unjustly identifying them all as Nazi collaborators and assigning each of them a fabricated crime. If I signed this, would my testimony then be used as proof that they committed these crimes? Could my confession sentence these people to death?

"I can't sign this," I told her.

"Trust me, they will go easier on you if you sign it," said Galina.

"I am not a collaborator, and you know it. Do you really think that Anya, the priest's wife, destroyed Soviet property? All those people you accuse of being Nazis, it's simply not true. I won't be a part of this."

She took the paper from me, then picked up the pail and slowly poured water over my head. It was icy cold and chilled me to the bone, but as it slowly coursed over me, I opened my mouth and swallowed as much as I could. The cold, fresh water felt glorious on my parched tongue. It was a small victory, as Mama would say.

"This isn't the last interrogation," said Galina. "You will sign that confession."

With the empty pail in one hand and the confessions in the other, she stomped back up the stairs.

The icy water soaked through my clothing and threw me into a fit of uncontrollable shivers, but Galina had forgotten to tie my hands back up. I squeezed as much water as I could from my hair and shirt.

Once the door slammed shut, Sophie said from her cell, "That was a really stupid thing to do, Krystia."

"You don't even know what you signed," I responded through chattering teeth. "That confession could haunt you for the rest of your life."

"Well, at least I'll have a life," said Sophie. "They'll release me now."

"Don't count on it," said Mychailo. "I signed mine just to make this torture stop."

"Does your confession implicate anyone else?" I asked him.

He lowered his voice and spoke softly in Ruthenian, an old country dialect not likely to be understood if our

Russians were eavesdropping. "The people named in my confession are already dead," he whispered. "A sad victory for me. At least they can't be hurt anymore."

"What do you think will happen to you now?" I asked Mychailo.

"Who knows?" he responded. "But anything's better than . . ."

The door upstairs opened again, and Galina reappeared. With an angry look on her face, she stepped over to me and loosened the ropes from my waist and feet. "You're coming with me," she said gruffly.

I tried to stand, but I had been tied up for so long that my knees crumpled and I fell. Galina grabbed me by the waistband and roughly pulled me to my feet. She practically carried me as I stumbled up the staircase.

The kitchen was permeated with an intense smell of onion and freshly peeled raw potatoes, and my stomach groaned with hunger. Galina propelled me out of the kitchen, through a hallway, and into the office area at the front of the mansion. The blackout blinds on the windows were pulled down so I had no idea whether it was day or night. She didn't stop there though, but pushed me toward the exit.

The guards at the door rolled up the barbed wire barricade so that we could walk through to the courtyard.

The sun enveloped me in its warmth and hurt my eyes with its brilliance. It felt so good to be outside. Was she letting me go?

But then my eyes adjusted to the light, and I understood Galina's sinister plan.

Maria was in the courtyard too. Her hands were tied behind her back, and she stood against the stone wall, looking frightened and pale. Lined up across from her were the two NKVD officers and the man in the blood-spattered undershirt. Each of them aimed their rifles at my sister's head.

Maria's eyes were glued to the firing squad, but then she noticed me.

Our eyes met.

"Sign your confession," said Galina. "Or your sister will be shot."

"Please don't hurt her!" I screamed.

I tried to run to Maria. If they were going to shoot her, they could shoot me too. Galina caught me by the waistband and held me in place.

My eyes locked on my sister's again, and I gasped for breath. I could not let them kill her, but I could not sign a confession that would cause the death of many more innocent people. As I stared at Maria, I saw a bit of blue cloth poking out of her pocket.

Mama.

"Don't sign it," shouted Maria in a surprisingly calm voice. She looked at Galina and said, "Krystia is just a simple girl who cleaned houses during the war. She can't tell you anything of use."

As I watched Maria boldly standing up to Galina and an execution squad, an image of Mama filled my mind. Mama defiant against the Nazi commandant in our town. But then also Mama's corpse swinging from a noose in the town square. I felt a great weight on my shoulders. If I made a false confession against those in our town who were working with the Ukrainian Insurgent Army, there would be many people swinging from nooses in the town square. But if I didn't sign it, my sister would be shot.

No matter what I did, I would have blood on my hands.

As I stared at my sister, I was struck by her maturity and poise. Yes, she would always be my baby sister, but she was also a young woman quite capable of making her own decisions. Before she'd run away with Nathan, she was my baby sister in every way, frightened of her own shadow, yet here she was calmly facing a firing squad, begging me not to sign the confession.

Awed by my sister's strength, I turned to Galina and said, "I will not sign your false confession."

I turned back to meet Maria's gaze. With her eyes

locked on mine, she closed her eyes slowly, then opened them again.

"I love you, Maria!" I shouted.

Galina muttered something under her breath, then pushed me roughly toward the mansion entrance. When we got inside she kicked me, and I fell onto my hands and knees inside the house.

Sharp staccato shots sounded from outside.

"No! Maria!"

I jumped off the floor and ran to the door. "My sister," I cried. "Let me out."

"It's a bit too late for that, don't you think?" said Galina.

I pushed past her. The two guards at the door tried to stop me, but I slipped out of their grip.

"Maria!" I cried.

She was crumpled on the ground, but as I got closer, I realized there were no blotches of blood. They had faked an execution. Her chest heaved, and she lifted her face from the ground, but she couldn't push herself back up because her hands were tied behind her back. I wrapped my arms around her waist and pulled her to her feet.

We were just one barbed wire barrier away from escaping this interrogation house. I ran toward the entrance, practically carrying Maria. I didn't stop to think what the guards might do to us if we were able to get through the barrier. I had only one thing on my mind—to get my sister out of this place.

But then a grip like steel landed on my shoulder. I turned. The man with the bloodied undershirt.

He grabbed Maria from my arms and tossed her to the ground. He lifted me up and threw me over his shoulder as if I were a sack of flour. As I kicked and hit him, I craned my neck to see what was happening to Maria. Galina had pulled Maria to her feet and was now gripping her by her bound hands and leading her into the mansion just a few meters behind me.

The man carried me through to the kitchen, then dropped me roughly on the floor. I was weak from the shock of my sister's near execution, but I stumbled to my feet and leaned against the wall for support. He opened the basement door and grabbed my arm, pushing me down the stairs in front of him, then he wordlessly shoved me back in my cell. He clanged the door shut behind me and stomped back up the stairs.

I curled into a ball on the metal cot and wept, not just from relief that my sister still lived but from exhaustion and dread of what would happen next.

CHAPTER EIGHTEEN– MY PAPERS

MARIA

I could tell that Galina was furious with both me and Krystia as she practically dragged me back to the holding room under the stairs. She opened the door, removed my handcuffs, then pushed me in.

I rubbed my wrists, trying to get the circulation back. Galina slammed the door and stomped away.

No one else was in the room. Where was Finn?

I leaned my back against the wall and took a deep shuddering breath. My whole body felt as if it were made out of jelly, and I slid down to the ground. I flopped onto my back and just lay there, staring at the light bulb overhead. Chill permeated my back from the floor, and I didn't even mind: It was a sign that I was still alive. I tried to calm my pounding heart and tried to slow the thoughts that raced through my mind.

It was not a pleasant experience to stand in front of an execution squad, but there is a certain exhilaration that comes with surviving an execution.

And I had seen my sister! Krystia was dirty, disheveled, and thin, but she looked defiant. I was so relieved to know that she was alive! And now I also knew for sure that she was being held in the basement, just as Finn and I had suspected.

And I was so proud of her that she didn't sign the confession. The Soviets were using that old technique of playing one family member off the other. Didn't they realize we couldn't be tricked like that? Krystia and I both knew that it was better to die than to betray more innocents. It was the only way to make the killing stop.

I lay on the floor for a very long time and counted my blessings:

Krystia was alive, and I knew where she was.

Galina put me here instead of back in the interrogation room. Did that mean the questioning would stop?

I had recently eaten potatoes and had some water.

I'd survived a mock execution!

And one more blessing: I was in a room with a toilet.

There was nothing I could do while I was locked up

all alone in this cell, except to make sure that I was as strong and alert as possible for whatever might come next. That meant getting some sleep without freezing, so I got up from the floor and paced back and forth to warm up. Then I got back down on the floor, curled into a ball, and tried to get some sleep.

As I huddled on the floor with my eyes closed, thoughts raced through my mind. My situation seemed better than Krystia's. For whatever reason, they were focusing on her and not me. I had only one room between me and the outside, but she had stairs and more rooms to get through. And even if we got out, what then? I had no idea where the border of this Soviet zone ended and no idea of how to get back to the Americans. It seemed impossible, but I wasn't about to give up.

What I really wanted was someone to talk to. If Nathan were still with me, we might have figured something out. Just the thought of him made my heart ache. It was the hardest decision of my life, to insist that he escape to Switzerland and leave me behind, but if he hadn't done that he wouldn't have survived. And I couldn't go with him because otherwise I would have lost Krystia.

And I was not about to lose Krystia now.

I didn't know how, but we'd get out of this. Both of us together, either dead or alive.

The floor was chilling me, so I turned on my other side. My thoughts still swirled. What about Finn? Was he being interrogated right now? How I wished that he were in this holding cell with me. That way I would at least know that he was okay. And maybe together we could figure out a way to escape, and to get Krystia out.

Did I fall asleep? I must have, because all at once, I jolted awake at the sound of the door being unlocked.

It wasn't Galina. And it wasn't the man with the bloodied undershirt. This time it was the NKVD woman, with an impatient expression on her face. I was cold through and through, but I scrambled to my feet and forced my mind to wake up and pay attention.

This woman regarded me with her cold and bored eyes. "You're being released," she said. And she handed me what appeared to be my papers!

Released? It seemed too good to be true. Was this another trick? She crooked her finger to indicate that I should follow her, so I stepped behind her with apprehension, and she led me out into the office area.

I nearly fainted from the intensely delicious scent of garlic, yeast, and meat. On each soldier's desk was a plate of aromatic piroshki—little deep-fried buns stuffed with ground meat. My stomach gurgled with hunger at the sight of them, yet it seemed that the interrogators themselves hardly appreciated their treat—the piroshki were half-eaten and drying out on their desks.

Only the NKVD woman's plate was empty, so I guessed she'd wolfed it all down before getting me from my cell. If I were her, I would have done the same thing. Galina didn't look up as we passed. She ignored me and her food as she pounded on her typewriter as if she were beating it.

"Let us pass," said the NKVD woman to the men who guarded the entrance. They moved the barbed wire so we could get through.

As we walked through the courtyard, I glanced at the spot where I had stood for my mock execution, and a shudder ran down my spine. I followed the NKVD woman to the guards who stood at the double-doored entrance in the stone wall. "This one's being released," she said.

They opened one door just enough to let me slip through. She stepped out with me, then grabbed my identity papers. At first, I thought this had all been a cruel ploy and I'd be marched back in, but she flipped through the papers and turned them to a page at the back where a whole new section had been typewritten in Russian. "You'll see here that you are to report to Work Unit Seven," she said. "Tomorrow morning, be in front of the town hall at six a.m. They will issue you a ration card."

"But how will I find the town hall?" I asked. "Everything's rubble."

"Just ask a local, and they'll show you," she said. Then she turned and stepped back through the door.

As I stood there alone in the street, on the other side of the stone wall, I was jubilant but also confused. I was so relieved to be out of that horrible house, but I was still tied to it because Krystia was there. I couldn't leave until I could get her out.

I flipped through my papers to ensure I had them all. My passport from the Reich was there, and so were the work papers from the Huber farm. I also still had the most important document of all: the letter from the Americans identifying me as a refugee, and now I saw that a red stamp and Russian typewriting had been added to the other side of this document: *Report for Obligatory Labor Service: Work Unit 7. 6:00 a.m. daily until deportation to Soviet interior scheduled.*

When we had arrived, I had seen work crews clearing out rubble. They'd looked like prisoners, overworked and starving. Was this the kind of work unit I had been assigned to? How would I save Krystia if I was forced into labor under the watchful eye of Soviets all day long? And deportation to the Soviet interior? That did not sound good. Were they planning on sending me to a slave camp in Siberia? How would I ever save Krystia if they sent me away?

CHAPTER NINETEEN– THREE GOOD THINGS

KRYSTIA

I had no idea how long I had been curled in a ball in my cell. The near execution of my sister played over and over in my mind. Maria was alive, but where was she now? I had to find her, to get her to safety. And what about my confession? Would they stop trying to get me to sign it now? That horrible Galina thought she could play Maria and me against each other. She clearly underestimated us, and that was a good thing.

And another good thing? We were two strong sisters. Neither of us would tell them anything useful.

I wondered if it was Galina who thought up the mock execution in the first place. She seemed to be a creative interrogator, and she was obviously good at it. After all, both Mychailo and Sophie signed their confessions. A shiver ran down my spine as I thought of how she tried to terrorize me with that dog. If it hadn't been for meeting Max, her technique might have worked on me.

The man with the bloodied undershirt looked more formidable, but I far preferred him over Galina. And as luck would have it, the door upstairs opened, and it was his heavy boots that sounded on the staircase. He stepped into our corridor and stopped in front of Mychailo's cell. I smashed my face against the bars, and while I couldn't see much, a steamy scent of potato and onion was in the air. When he stepped in front of my cell, I nearly swooned with joy. He gave me a mug holding a hot boiled potato with water and boiled onion. I slurped up the onion and water first, then dumped the potato onto my palm, relishing its warmth. I handed the mug back to the man.

"Thank you," I said.

He grunted.

And then I sat down on my cot with the potato cupped carefully in my hands as if it were a bird that could fly away. This potato was a precious thing. It gave me warmth and sustenance, but even more important than that, it gave me hope for the future. If they meant to kill me, they wouldn't waste food on me, would they?

I nibbled at the edge of my potato and groaned with pleasure as I slowly chewed and swallowed it down.

CHAPTER TWENTY-
BIRGIT
MARIA

As I stood in the street, my mind a jumble of questions and worries, a warm hand gripped my elbow and maneuvered me away from the front of the mansion.

"This isn't a good place to loiter," said an oddly familiar voice. It was the kerchiefed woman who had brought the watery soup to our cell. Only now she was wearing a different kerchief and a jacket over her dress. Had it not been for her voice, I wouldn't have recognized her.

"What are you doing?" I asked her, alarmed.

"Taking you to someplace that's safer," she said.

We walked together in silence, weaving through a maze of what used to be city streets, stepping around holes and over mounds of rubble. Should I trust her? She had a job supplying the interrogators with food, after all. Maybe she was going to trick me. But then I remembered the words she said to us, the words that made Galina sneer. She'd said, "May God be with each of you."

If she were a communist or a Nazi, she wouldn't have said that because they don't believe in God. I decided to trust her—for the moment.

"Here we are," she said, pausing in front of a bent metal roof that had collapsed on top of a pyramid of crushed bricks and shattered wooden beams.

I stood beside her, puzzled. This house looked no different from any of the other ruined buildings that we had passed, but she got down on her hands and knees and tugged at a metal cauldron that seemed to be stuck at the base of the rubble.

She turned to me and said, "You could help, you know."

I got down beside her. "What is it that you want me to do?" I asked.

"Hold that beam steady while I pull out the pot," she said.

It seemed to be a strange thing to do, but who was I to argue? I had no idea what was going on. I pushed up on the beam, holding it steady while she yanked at the cauldron. All at once, the cauldron gave way, revealing a dark hole in the rubble big enough for a person to get into. And while a couple of bricks around the hole had tumbled down when the cauldron was removed, the rest of the structure remained solid.

"This is the way in."

While facing me, she lay flat on her belly and shimmied in feetfirst. Her kerchiefed head disappeared, and then her arms and hands. There was a scraping sound, then a clunk.

"Hold on to the cauldron as you enter so it covers the hole up again," her voice echoed through the hole. "But let go of it as soon as you feel it falling toward you."

I did as she said, getting onto my belly, then grabbing on to the cauldron and easing myself feetfirst into the hole. I slowly wiggled downward. When I was halfway in, I felt her arms around my knees, and she steadied me. I was grateful for that. This whole situation was strange and scary.

When just my hands and forearms still stuck out of the hole, I let go of the cauldron and fell. My feet touched the ground with a thump, and the cauldron rattled into place.

I was surrounded by shadows and a scattering of light filtering through cracks from above. We were standing on the earthen floor of a root cellar that seemed surprisingly undamaged. The walls were solid concrete block, and above us were wide metal beams that kept the mounds of debris from collapsing in on us. In a heavy rain I'm sure this shelter would get drenched, but the space was in such good shape that there were even some intact shelves lining one of the walls. There was a small rectangular hearth made of broken bricks near the center of the room with pots stacked beside it and bits of burnt wood and coal inside.

There was a wooden door balanced on stacks of bricks that served as a table. Around it were upturned pails that looked to be used as chairs.

As my eyes adjusted, I saw pillows and blankets stacked neatly in a hamper and boxes stored in a corner.

"We haven't been formally introduced," said the woman. "My name is Birgit Ziegler. Are you Maria, Krystia, or Sophie?"

"I . . . I'm Maria," I said. "How do you know about me, Krystia, and Sophie?"

"From Finn," she said.

"Finn's here?" I asked, looking around.

"He'll likely be back before it gets dark," she said. "We've been taking turns keeping watch on the NKVD interrogation house ever since he was released."

I sat down on one of the upturned pails and tried to sort out my new reality. "Do you live down here?" I asked.

"Sometimes." Her eyes darted around, as if she were looking for something. "Are you hungry?"

"I don't need to eat," I said.

"Will you be fine on your own for a while down here?" Birgit asked.

I looked at her, startled. I hardly knew her, and now she was leaving me in her secret hiding place?

"Where are you going?" I asked her.

"I need to barter for some good-quality food on the black market—something the interrogators will enjoy eating," she said.

"Are you sure you want me staying down here? You barely know me."

"Just stay," she said. "You'll get lost if you go up there on your own. I'll be back as soon as I can, and Finn might be back before that."

I thought she was going to leave, but instead she paused and looked me up and down with a frown. "You stick out like a sore thumb."

"What do you mean?" I asked.

"If anyone sees you, you'll be picked up on the spot. The Soviets are on the lookout for two types of people: Nazi officers on the run, and Slavs who survived Nazi imprisonment—former slave laborers and prisoners of war."

I pulled out my refugee papers and showed them to her, pointing at the words typed in Russian. "I've already been picked up. I've been assigned to a temporary work group and deportation to the Soviet Union."

"You're not going to show up for that," Birgit said.

"But I won't get a ration card if I don't report to the town hall," I said.

"Just because you get a ration card doesn't mean you'll get much food," she said. "And if you report for work, you'll be written into the system. The administration of this zone is so disorganized right now that as long as you disappear, they'll hardly notice."

"So I'm just supposed to stay down here?" I asked.

"That's not what I mean," said Birgit. "You need to look like a German civilian, a local, instead of a refugee."

"And how am I supposed to do that?" I asked.

"Finn blends in with the locals around here. His clothing may be worn and dusty, but it's clean enough and decent-looking. And he cleaned himself up once he was released. You, on the other hand, are wearing rags. And you're filthy."

My face got hot with embarrassment, and I crossed my arms over my chest. "They don't exactly let you take a bath in the interrogation house," I said. "And I've been living on the road, sleeping in the open, for months."

"Child, I'm not blaming you," said Birgit. "I just don't want you to draw attention to yourself."

She pointed to a box in the corner. "Feel free to look in there for something more presentable, and if you need it, there's a sewing kit on the shelf. It will give you something to do while I'm gone."

Birgit grabbed a jar and a milk pitcher from the shelf, then set them and a spoon on the table. "Here's boiled water and an opened jar of honey. If you're hungry, have some honey, but don't open any of the other food. We try to have only one item of food open at any time because we don't want to attract insects. And try to have no more than a glass of water, because this is all the drinking water we have right now."

After the horrible treatment at the NKVD house, Birgit's trust and kindness was almost overwhelming, and I had to force myself not to burst into tears.

"Thank you," I said.

"Oh, child," she said, her own voice getting hoarse with tears. "You would have done the same for me." She pointed to a bar of soap and basin on the shelf. "Grab the basin, and I'll show you how you can get cleaned up."

She wove her way down a corridor through the rubble, and I kept close behind her. Soon we were in a second dirt-floored basement space, but this one was open to the sky. It was protected on all sides by sturdy concrete walls sunken into the ground, and even though anyone who walked by could look down into it, I didn't think many people *could* walk by because of all the rubble stacked around it. There was a barrel nestled up against one of the concrete walls with a wide spout attached to collect rainwater that would run off a portion of an intact roof above it. Leaning up against another wall was a stepladder.

"Why didn't we come down the stepladder instead of through the hole?" I asked.

Birgit smiled. "We don't want to draw attention to our hiding place," she said. "If we used the ladder all the time, there would be more chance that people would notice. Besides, dropping through the hole is a quick way of getting in."

I nodded, marveling at how she thought through everything.

Birgit pointed to the water barrel. "Don't drink that water," she said. "It's got all the runoff from the bombs and smoke and damage. But it's good enough to wash with."

She took off her jacket and switched her headscarf so she was wearing the one she'd worn in the interrogation house. And then she walked over to the ladder and began to climb. "I'll be back as soon as I can."

I watched her disappear through the debris.

I was excited about the prospect of getting clean. How long had it been since I'd had a bath? Months! But I didn't want to wash myself out here in the open, so I filled the basin with water and retraced my steps back through to the main cellar.

As I set the water and soap on the table, I looked down at my jacket and blouse and skirt and realized just how disgustingly grimy they were, but how could I wash them when I had nothing else to change into?

I plunged my hands into the rainwater and swirled them around the basin, then grabbed the bar of soap and lathered it up, scrubbing underneath my fingernails and all over my palms and wrists and arms. It felt so glorious to have the opportunity to wash. Once my hands and arms were so pink and clean that they didn't look like mine anymore, I lathered up soap on my face, scrubbing my neck and behind my ears. It was so great to get the accumulated grime off that I didn't even care when the soap stung my eyes. As I splashed my face to get the last of the soapsuds off, I realized that the water in the basin was a scummy brown. I took it to the outside cellar, dumped it out, and refilled my basin.

The next thing I tackled was my hair. I began by trying to wet it a bit at a time with handfuls of water but finally just dunked my whole head into the basin and then rubbed the bar of soap directly on my scalp until I got a good lather. It felt so good to scrub the dirt and lice powder and dried scabs from old bug bites out of my hair. I ran my fingers through the suds and tried to take out the worst of the tangles. My hair was a ball of knots and full of soapy residue, but that was preferable to all the dirt. I went back to the open cellar and knelt below the spigot in the rain barrel and rinsed and rinsed until my hair squeaked. I stood up and shook my head, watching the droplets of water flying in the fresh air and sunlight. For the first time in a long time, I felt human.

With water streaming down my face and back, I got another fresh basin of rainwater and set it on the table. Even though my clothing was almost completely drenched from my wet hair, I didn't want to get undressed until I could find something clean to change into.

Then I remembered my papers.

Were they now wet and ruined from washing my hair?

I reached into my pocket and pulled out the scrap of blue cloth that reminded me of Mama. I gave it a kiss and set it on the table. Next, I took my papers out and set them on the table, then very gently, I opened each one and breathed a sigh of relief. Only the edges had gotten wet, and none of the ink had been disturbed. I smoothed them out flat with my hands and let them dry on the table.

I opened the box that Birgit had pointed out to me. On the top were carefully folded hand towels and cloth diapers, so I took out the largest cloth square and wrapped it around my hair. My hand brushed over the next item, which felt like a good-quality woolen coat, but when I pulled it out, I couldn't help but groan. It was the jacket to a Nazi officer's uniform. Reich jackets, helmets, and insignia were as common as rain in all the destruction and rubble these days. As soon as the Nazis were defeated, Reich soldiers had flung off any piece of clothing that could identify them as the enemy and tried to mingle in as civilians. It was sickening.

I looked down at my own filthy and threadbare rags. They barely held together, but they were preferable to a Nazi jacket. Still, my fingers lingered on the jacket. The uniform material was of excellent quality. It could be ripped apart, maybe even dyed, and made into other pieces of clothing, although not by me and not right now.

Deeper into the box I found a woman's party dress and some baby clothing. My heart ached at the thought of these lives interrupted, but neither of the items was useful to me. There were also some books, all in German. There were several copies of Hitler's book, *Mein Kampf,* which didn't surprise me. It had been mandatory reading for Germans. Now they'd be good for starting a fire or stuffing into my shoes for warmth.

Just below the books were half a dozen or so folded Nazi flags. These had been proudly displayed on nearly every German's house for most of the war, but now they'd been discarded as humiliating reminders of false pride. I shook one out and held it up. If I couldn't find anything else, this would be big enough to cover me up while I washed my clothing and set it out to dry. I'd have to be very desperate to do that though, because it would be awful if anyone came down here while I was wrapped up in a Nazi flag.

Underneath the flags was one carefully folded uniform of the League of German Girls. I shook out the leather-belted blue paneled skirt and held it up, but it was way too big. I unfolded the white blouse that went with it and held it up to my chest. It was unadorned except for a crest on the left shoulder, but the blouse was also too big. The items were both clean and of good material, but even if I took the crest off and sized it all down, a white blouse with a dark blue skirt couldn't be anything but a Hitler Girl uniform. On the other hand, I had to put on something while my own clothing was drying, and this was better than wrapping myself up in a Nazi flag. I set the clothes out on the table.

It took several more basins of water, but once I had thoroughly scrubbed myself from top to toe and rinsed myself off, I felt wonderful. I slipped on the huge uniform, folding the waist of the skirt and wrapping the leather belt around my waist twice to keep it from falling off.

I scrubbed my old clothing in soapy water, but the fabric was so fragile that it began to dissolve in my hands. I held up my blouse and gasped. It was nothing but ribbons of cloth now. My skirt and underwear were ruined.

I searched through the box again and took out the party dress. I removed the Hitler Girl clothing and put on the dress. I found the sewing kit on one of the shelves and opened it—scissors, black thread, and a needle. It was all I needed. I took the outfit, the sewing kit, and a pail to sit on out to the sunny root cellar and got to work. When I spread the skirt flat on the ground and smoothed out the panels—eight of them—I realized that it was a full circle. This was a lot of material. I snipped off the waistband and took the stitching out of a couple of the panels. It took just two of the panels to make a simple shift-style dress for myself. I stitched in a single deep pocket inside at the waist, then basted down the neck opening and the arm-holes so they wouldn't fray, and cut off two strips with the leftover material: one for a belt and one to tie my hair back with. I would have liked to have a blouse to wear under-neath, but I didn't want it to be white, because that would still make me look too much like a Hitler Girl.

I went back into the main root cellar and slipped off the party dress, then put on the new blue shift and tied the cloth belt. It seemed to fit well, even if my arms were a bit chilly.

And then I took another look at the party dress. It was two layers—a gauzy pink floral pattern on the top and a satiny pink liner underneath. The dress was sleeveless, but there was enough satiny material in the skirt to make a blouse with. I made it tunic-style with long bell sleeves and carefully hemmed the pink edges with the black thread. When it was finished, I admired my handiwork. This pink blouse looked nothing like a Nazi uniform, and it would entirely change the look of my new blue shift.

I slipped off the shift, put on the blouse, then put the shift back on. There was one last thing that I needed, and that was underpants. I went back to the box and sorted through the possibilities. I could make a pair of underwear out of the diaper material if I had to, or from the dishcloths, but both those items would be useful to someone as they were. Then I pulled out one of the Nazi flags. This was of no use to anyone in its present state. The swastika in the middle was a stiff material, but the red fabric that made the background was a soft and sturdy wool. I snipped off a section of the red and shaped it like diaper-style panties that could be tied at the sides. As I slipped my new red panties on and tied them up, I couldn't help but smile. It made me very happy to use the Nazi flag this way. It felt wonderful to be in all fresh clothing, and as I looked down at myself, I could hardly believe that it was me. The only thing that had stayed the same were my worn-out shoes.

But as I reveled in my new clothing and cleanliness, my

heart ached at the thought of Krystia, still in the interrogation house. I picked up the blue cloth and the remnants of the party dress. "How I wish that you could wear new clothing too, Krystia," I whispered under my breath.

And then I thought, *Why can't she?* Krystia might not be with me yet, but I was determined to save her. Krystia's clothing was in as bad shape as mine. As I set to work on a second shift and blouse, both just a little bit bigger than my own, I thought of Mama and all the items she had altered and shaped as our clothing became too ragged to wear. She'd taught me the art of careful cutting and fine stitching, and I was so grateful for that. I shaped a second pair of underpants out of the Nazi flag. I held them all up to admire, then folded all the items carefully and put them away. I could hardly wait to give them to my sister.

There was still a good quantity of cloth left from the Jugend skirt. I thought of Sophie and how she might also need new clothing. She was bigger than me or Krystia though, and I didn't want to ruin this precious cloth by guessing and then cutting it too small. In the end I made the leftovers into a simple wraparound skirt and wrap blouse because the size was adjustable.

After that, I was very tired. I was hungry too, but I felt awkward about eating any of the honey. I had already used so much of Birgit's soap and rainwater, and I was wearing clothing from things that she had scavenged. It seemed greedy for me to want more than that, even though my stomach growled at the thought of a spoonful of honey. But what if eating one spoonful of it made me even hungrier? What if I ended up eating more than Birgit thought I should? It was better just to wait and eat when Birgit got back. I poured myself half a cup of drinking water from the jug and savored that instead. I sat on one of the upturned pails and laid my head on the door that served as a table. The room got gradually darker, and I fell asleep.

I was awoken by the sound of metal scraping on brick. Someone was removing the cauldron from the entrance to the root cellar.

I stood beneath it and looked up, waiting and watching, hoping that it was either Finn or Birgit and not a stranger. The cauldron disappeared, and in its place was a circle of blue-black twilight.

A burlap bag careened through the opening, nearly hitting my head.

"Careful," I screamed, jumping out of the way and nearly tripping over the hearth. The bag plopped onto the floor.

Through a halo of twilight, Finn's red hair and pale face appeared. "Who's there?" he shouted.

"It's me, Maria."

Finn's face broke out into a grin. "Maria! I'll be right down."

There was a scratching and scrambling from above, and then Finn's shoes appeared.

"Do you want me to help you?" I asked.

"No," he said. "Just stay clear."

I grabbed the neck of the burlap bag and pulled it over to the table. Finn jumped down, lithe as a cat, and the cauldron settled into its place above us, plunging us back into darkness. There was a whoosh of a match, and the root cellar was illuminated. Finn lit a candle, then blew out the match.

It was clear to me that Finn had also bathed. No lice powder dulled his hair, plus his face and hands were so clean they were almost pink.

He rushed over to me and wrapped me in a bear hug. "I'm so glad to see you, Maria," he said. Then he held me at arm's length and looked at me from head to toe. "This is a new getup," he said. "Nice and clean too."

"My clothing fell apart when I tried to wash it," I told him. "I made this out of a Jugend skirt."

He smiled at that and said, "You've done a good job of transforming it." But then his eyebrows knitted with concern. "We heard the shots."

164

"It was a mock execution," I said. "They told Krystia they'd shoot me unless she signed their confession."

"She signed it?" he asked.

"No. They made her think I was executed. But she knows I'm still alive."

"Has she been moved from the interrogation house yet?" Finn asked.

"Moved?" I said, confused. "Where else would she be? No, she's in the basement."

"People around here said the Soviets have been taking prisoners to a Nazi death camp just outside of town."

I froze. Finn's words made no sense.

"The death camps have been liberated," I said. "You and I both know that."

"You're right," said Finn. "But the Nazi camps around here are now being used by the NKVD. No one stays at the interrogation house for long."

My knees went weak. I collapsed onto an upturned pail. "So Krystia could be sent to one of those camps any time now?"

"That's right," said Finn.

"We have to rescue her."

"You think I don't know that?" he said. "Why do you think I haven't escaped from here yet?"

CHAPTER TWENTY-ONE-
ANTHEM
KRYSTIA

The light from the one bulb in my cell gave me a grinding headache, but being in a too-bright room was better than being plunged into darkness. Besides, having a headache couldn't shake the exhilaration I felt knowing that Maria was alive! The interrogators had tried their best to get us to give up names, but we had both held firm. And awful as this cell was, it was far better than being tied to that chair. Added to my gratitude list was that one glorious steaming potato. And another thing I was grateful for? The man with the bloodied shirt brought us all another mug of sludgy water. Living under the Nazis' terror was a great way to prepare for Soviet torture.

After the three of us had our drink of gray water and

the man had gone back upstairs, Mychailo said, "What do you think they color the water with?"

That made me smile, and Sophie snorted a laugh.

"A handful of dirt?" I said.

"Maybe," said Mychailo.

"So," he continued, "tell me about the most delicious meal you've ever had."

"I can tell you that one," said Sophie. "It was when my brother Otto came home from the front at Christmas. We were sent a führer's package, which was extra rations of meat, fat, sugar, and flour. We made tarts, tortes, candies, cookies, and puddings. But the best part was the wiener schnitzel—veal pounded thin, breaded, and deep-fried— and rösti, fried potato topped with eggs and onions."

As she spoke, my hands clenched in anger. This was a story I was familiar with, but from Maria's point of view. Maria was the one who made the food while on a starvation diet herself. She had been forced to make linzer cookies cut into the shape of swastikas. Christmas? No. What Hitler Girl would celebrate the birth of Jesus, a Jew? Sophie was talking about her Rauhnacht—rough night— celebration, with her tree decorated in trinkets of Jews hanging from scaffolds.

My mind filled with the image of the warehouse in

our town, stuffed to the brim, where the Nazis stored all the food and goods that they stole from the townspeople. How many führer's packages did our stolen food make?

"Let me tell you about my most delicious meal," I said. "Our food had long been confiscated by the Nazis, and I was so hungry that I would go up to the loft and chew on hay. Mama bartered with a farmer for an old, scrawny cow. We slaughtered it in secret, hid a lot of the meat, and shared it with our starving friends. That first serving of roast beef was the most delectable meal ever."

"That was audacious," said Mychailo. "You didn't get caught?"

"A German civilian reported us," I said. "The Nazis ransacked our house but never found the hidden packages of meat."

"That's great," said Mychailo.

"They fined us anyway," I said. "And it was such a crushing fine that Mama had to sell most of our meat to pay the fine. She rode the rails into Lviv with the meat hidden under her clothes. She sold it to restaurants that catered to the Nazis."

"I hope they choked on it," said Mychailo, laughing.

"That's not very funny," said Sophie.

We were all silent for a few moments, but then Mychailo spoke.

"I'll tell you about my most delicious meal," he said. "This was after my parents were killed."

"How did they die?" I asked.

"The Nazis came to our town and burned the whole thing down. Practically everyone died, including my parents and sisters. I had been in the woods looking for food when it happened, so I escaped. I found the bodies of my family though, and that was awful."

"This doesn't sound like the story of a best meal," said Sophie.

"I'm getting to that," said Mychailo. "I fled but was captured by the Nazis and sent to work on a German farm. They fed me practically nothing and made me live in the barn with the animals."

"Same as my sister," I said. "On Sophie's farm." I couldn't help myself.

"Oh, shut up," said Sophie.

"Anyway, one day, I happened upon an egg. One of their chickens had laid an egg in the grass and no one noticed. I picked it up and hid it in my pocket. I was able to get behind the barn. When no one was looking, I cracked it raw into my mouth and swallowed it down. It was the most delicious meal I've ever had."

I could taste the egg myself from Mychailo's description. A raw egg wasn't something that I would have ever eaten before the war, but it was a small and filling food to steal when you were starving. "Did you get caught?" I asked.

"I did," said Mychailo. "Their little daughter found the broken shell behind the barn. They beat me within an inch of my life, but it was worth it."

"A nice fresh raw egg would go down nicely just about now," I said.

"You're right about that," said Sophie. "How did you end up here, Mychailo?"

"A few months ago, I escaped from that farm. There was no home to go back to, so I came here instead. This area wasn't even in the Soviet zone then. A few weeks ago, the Soviets picked me off the street in a random check. They think I was with the Underground in Belarus."

"Why did you come here of all places?" I asked.

Mychailo didn't answer. It took me a moment to realize why. There had to be someone in the area he knew, and he couldn't let the Soviets know who they were. I could have kicked myself for asking such a dumb question.

"Who can sing the Soviet national anthem?" I said, out of nowhere, but just to change the subject. At least if we had eavesdroppers, they would like that.

Sophie didn't know the words, but Mychailo and I did. We had both suffered under two years of Soviet occupation before the Nazis, after all. As we both sang the first verse, I stifled my urge to gag.

Unbreakable union of freeborn republics
Great Russia has welded forever to stand!
Created in struggle by will of the peoples
United and mighty, our Soviet Union!

CHAPTER TWENTY-TWO–
LINZER COOKIES
MARIA

Finn opened the burlap sack. I looked inside. A tin of meat, brown twine wrapped in a ball, and a hammer. "Food," I said, holding up the tin.

"Everything's scarce here," he said. "It's not like in the American zone where the soldiers help civilians. Here, the Red Army soldiers are running around, taking what they want, and their officers don't seem to be able to stop them. Then some other Soviet group is disassembling German factories and shipping them to the Soviet Union. Total chaos."

I set the tin on the table beside the jar of honey and asked, "How did you get out of the NKVD house?"

"They released me shortly after they took you and me to separate rooms."

"Did they interrogate you?" I asked.

Finn shook his head. "They wanted my father, not me. Once he agreed to their terms, they let both of us go."

"What were their terms?" I asked.

"For Vater to work as a policeman for the Soviets."

"Why would the Soviets want a German policeman?" I asked.

"Nearly all the policemen here are German," he responded. "Most of the refugees don't speak Russian as their first language and the German locals don't understand Russian. Vater speaks both languages. He's supposed to stop refugees and locals from looting, even though the worst looters are actually Red Army soldiers, and they won't obey someone like Vater."

"But you're looting," I said, pointing to his sack. "Won't you get your father into trouble?"

"We pretend we don't know each other in public," said Finn.

"And he lives down here with you?" I asked.

Finn shook his head. "He's been assigned sleeping quarters in the old town hall."

"The town hall?" I said. I grabbed my refugee papers and handed them to Finn. "I'm supposed to report to a work unit at the town hall tomorrow morning, but Birgit said I shouldn't go."

Finn smoothed the papers out onto the table and read

the Russian words that had been typed onto the back. "'Obligatory Labor Service . . . deportation,'" he said. "Birgit's right. Don't go anywhere near the town hall."

"But it says right here that I have to." I poked my finger at the words on the paper.

"This entire area is in disarray," said Finn. "The NKVD and the Red Army are overwhelmed with work, and they don't seem to know what the other is doing half the time. They'll notice you more if you show up than if you stay away."

"Won't they just come after me?"

"If you show up, you're in trouble for sure. If they catch you, you're in trouble. Don't let them catch you," said Finn.

Easier said than done, I thought to myself.

Finn pointed to my outfit. "That will help you blend in better."

"I just need to blend in long enough to free my sister," I said.

Finn opened his mouth to respond, but there were more scraping noises from above.

The cauldron moved.

A cloth bag dropped down first, then a well-worn pair of women's shoes appeared and Birgit dropped to the floor.

"Meat," she said, spying the tin on the table. "Good find, Finn."

"Should we open it for dinner, or are you going to use it for the interrogators?" Finn asked.

"I've got one tin of meat saved for the interrogators, and that should be enough," she said.

"Should I open it now, then?" asked Finn.

"Wait a bit," said Birgit. "I ran into your father and told him about Maria. He'll be here soon and will join us."

Birgit grabbed the cloth bag she'd brought with her and opened it. She drew out half a loaf of rye bread and two shriveled carrots and set them on the table.

"Is that for us or for them?" asked Finn.

"Us, I think," she said.

"What did you end up bringing the interrogators to eat today?" Finn asked.

"I managed to purchase a tin of linzer cookies from an old lady in the street," she said.

Linzer cookies—two cookie wafers with raspberry jam in the middle. I knew from working at the Huber farm that these were Hitler's favorite cookie. And how could I forget being forced to make them into the shape of little swastikas?

"Did they like them?" he asked.

"They did," she said.

"Why do you bring the interrogators food?" I asked. "Is it just for the extra money, or do you do it so you can have access to better food for yourself as well?"

Birgit's eyebrows rose. "Didn't Finn tell you about my grandson?"

I shook my head.

"His name is Mychailo Karpovich. My daughter married a Belarussian. Everyone in her family except Mychailo was killed by the Nazis. He came here to live with me but was picked up in a random street check by the Soviets two weeks ago. He's a prisoner in the NKVD house too."

"But what does that have to do with bringing food to the interrogators?" I asked.

"It's a way for me to spy on them, also for me to gain their trust."

"Oh," I said. "I'm so sorry." My terrible assumptions made me feel like cringing, especially because she had treated me—a stranger—so kindly.

"I haven't seen him since he was arrested," said Birgit, tears welling up in her eyes. "Not in all the times I've been there, but I pray that he's still alive."

"There are many rooms for prisoners in that place," I said. "Two upstairs floors, the basement, and as you've seen for yourself, cells on the main floor."

"You're right," she said. "He could be anywhere in there." She sighed deeply.

I was about to ask for more information, but the scraping sound from above announced a new arrival.

It was Elias in a Soviet police uniform, bearing a bag of coal but not any food. He dropped the bag down through the opening, and then he came down himself. I was so thrilled to see him that I gave him a big hug.

"I'm relieved that you're out of that place, Maria," said Elias. "That means one less person to save and one more person to help with our plan."

"We'll talk while we eat," said Birgit. "We should celebrate Maria's arrival by opening the extra tin of meat that Finn found." She passed the tin over to Elias. "You can do the honors."

While Elias used a can opener on the tin, Birgit broke off a hunk of bread for each of us, and Finn grabbed the spoon.

"Since you're the newest to our group," Finn said, passing me the spoon, "you can have the first taste of meat."

Elias set the tin of meat on the table in front of me, and I scooped out a tiny bit of it and spread it on a piece of my bread. Before placing it on my tongue, I said, "Let us give thanks for this food and hope that it makes us strong enough to save our friends." I had no idea what was in the concoction, but it was thick with oil and seasoned with salt and garlic. Spread on the bread, it tasted heavenly and was satisfyingly filling.

After I had spread that first spoonful on the bread, I

passed the spoon to Finn, and once he had his share, he gave the spoon to Birgit, who then gave it to Elias. Finn filled a tin cup with water and passed it around too. We finished our meal in silence, savoring every mouthful.

As I picked up stray crumbs from the table and put them in my mouth, I surveyed the people around me: Birgit, almost a stranger, but I already trusted her with my life; Elias, who had proven himself to be reliable; and Finn, who was now my friend.

"How are we going to get Krystia, Mychailo, and the others out of the interrogation house?" I asked.

Elias took a sip of water. "We've been working toward that since Finn and I were released."

"Actually, I've been working on trying to get people out for a long time," said Birgit. "But it will work better now that I've got more people to help me."

"Tell me how supplying the interrogators with food is part of that plan," I asked her.

"We've managed to get sleeping capsules," said Elias. "The powder from inside the capsules can be mixed into the food."

"Sleeping capsules?" I asked. "How did you find something like that?"

"More easily than you might think," said Birgit. "A lot of people had these capsules around during the war.

I found half a bottle when I was scavenging a blown-up house."

"So how will this plan work?" I asked.

"Once the interrogators all fall asleep, we sneak in, open the cells, and everyone escapes," said Finn. "Our biggest challenge was to figure out a food that the powder could be put in, and a food that we could actually make."

I looked at Birgit and Elias, then Finn, and I remembered about the food I had seen on their desks. "Is that why you brought them piroshki the other day?" I asked.

Birgit nodded. "I've been bringing them all sorts of special treats when I'm able so they're not suspicious about what I bring. That's why they got linzer cookies today. I've got the ingredients for another batch of piroshki, and with your help and Finn's, we can make them early tomorrow morning, but this time we'll mix the sleeping powder into the meat. I'll bring them tomorrow, and they'll fall asleep. Then we can go in and open up the cells."

"Except not everybody liked the piroshki," I said.

"How could they not like them?" Birgit asked. "Meat, dough, deep-fried—what's not to like?"

"I have no idea," I said. "But most were half-eaten, sitting on their plates. I noticed because I would have loved to gobble them all down."

"Maybe it was the way you seasoned it," suggested Finn.

"But meat," said Birgit. "What a waste if they didn't like it."

"What ingredients do you have saved up?" I asked Birgit.

She listed them off with her fingers. "Yeast, flour, one onion, and I now have two carrots. And I've got another tin of meat saved up special."

"Does the sleeping powder change the taste of the food?" I asked.

"I don't know," said Birgit. "We don't have a way of testing it out ahead of time."

"Are the sleeping pills here?"

Birgit got up from the table and looked through one of the boxes. She came back a few minutes later with a pill bottle in her hand. She opened it and handed me a single yellow capsule that could be pulled apart in the middle.

I opened it up and sprinkled a few grains of white powder onto my palm. I tasted it with the tip of my tongue. "Very bitter," I said.

"Don't swallow that," said Finn, jumping up from the table to grab a rag. "Spit it into this."

"If it's bitter, the food needs to have a strong taste," said Elias.

"The piroshki have a strong taste," said Birgit. "But if

they didn't like them that much without the sleeping powder, they won't finish them if there's a bitter taste."

"With the powder being bitter, something savory wouldn't work so well, but a strong sweet taste would counteract the bitter," I said.

Birgit raised her eyebrows. "And they did like those linzer cookies."

"You can't make linzer cookies here though, can you?" I asked. "You don't have the ingredients."

"It's not just that," said Birgit. "We've only got the hearth for cooking. We can boil, fry, and deep-fry. That's it."

"Let me think about this," I said.

"Do it quickly," said Finn. "Our plan was to go in tomorrow."

CHAPTER TWENTY-THREE—THE LATCH
KRYSTIA

I paced back and forth in my cell, marveling at the fact that I was doing absolutely nothing, yet it felt like torture. As I paced, I worried and wondered about Maria's fate. And as I paced, I worried and wondered about my own.

I also worried and wondered about Mychailo and Sophie. Why were they still here? Their confessions were signed. Galina said they'd be getting out. So what was the delay? Would they be released, or would they be sent to a camp? I doubted they'd just get released after signing those damning confessions. Where would their next prison be? In Siberia?

My biggest worry was that the interrogators could be waiting for me to confess so they could ship us all out together. Or maybe execute us all together. What torture would they put me through next in order to get me to sign? So many people counted on me staying strong. I hoped and prayed that I could outlast the interrogators.

Just as that thought passed through my mind, the door upstairs opened, and light footsteps sounded on the stairs. I heard a metal clink as the person retrieved the cell key from the hook on the wall. Moments later, Galina appeared in our corridor.

I pushed my face to the bars to see what she was up to. She passed Mychailo's cell without a glance but then stopped at mine. She opened my door and grabbed my arm and pulled me to the open area with the interrogation chairs.

"Sit," she said.

And I did.

She retrieved some items from the staircase—a plate of what looked like cookies and papers that looked like the typed confession she was trying to get me to sign. She paced in front of me, holding the plate of cookies in one hand and the confession under her elbow.

She looked at me and smiled. "These are such a tasty treat," she said. "Linzer cookies. Did you know they were Hitler's favorites?"

She picked one up and popped it into her mouth. "Mmmm," she said. "Delicious."

She walked over to me and set the plate on my lap. My hands were not tied. I could have taken one of those cookies in a flash if I had wanted to, but I resisted the urge. My mouth watered at the very thought of those cookies, so I didn't look at the plate but instead stared into my interrogator's eyes. Did she really think I would sign away people's lives for a few bites of cookie?

She held the plate under my nose. The scent of linzer cookies filled my nostrils: aromatic raspberry jam enveloped between two thin, crisp, buttery, cinnamon-scented cookies. It took a huge amount of willpower to keep my eyes on the woman, and to not look down at the cookies. My stomach grumbled. More than anything I wanted to grab one of those cookies and shove it into my mouth.

"Mychailo and Sophie can each have a cookie too," she said. "They're very hungry, you know. All you have to do is sign."

"Comrade," I said in as respectful a voice as I could muster. "Thank you for defeating the Nazis. I hate their ideology as much as you do. But I will not sign your confession. What you've got typed there is not true."

She picked one of the cookies off the plate and held it up so close to my face that I could not look away. The raspberry jam oozed out of the center in a most delectable way, and the scent of almonds and vanilla mingled with the cinnamon and butter and a hint of lemon. I closed my eyes and held my breath.

I heard the cookie drop back onto the plate. I opened my eyes just in time to see her whoosh the plate away and put it back on the staircase.

"Go to your cell," she shouted.

I jumped from the chair and hurried down the corridor, with Galina chasing after me. She clanged the door shut with a jarring force, then stomped upstairs.

It took me a few minutes to realize that the lock had not engaged. My cell door was not latched shut.

CHAPTER TWENTY-FOUR—
BERRIES
MARIA

"Each day that goes by puts Mychailo, Krystia, and Sophie at greater risk," said Birgit, pacing.

"You're right," I said. "We can't waste time, but if you had gone in with the drugged piroshki, that would have been the end of it. You would have used up the sleeping pills, and not everyone would have fallen asleep. You would likely have been arrested and thrown into a cell."

Birgit sat down on one of the upturned pails. "You're right," she said. "But if at all possible, I still want to carry out our plan tomorrow."

"I agree with you," I said. "But we don't even know what food we're going to hide the sleeping powder in."

"Come scavenging with me tomorrow," said Finn. "We'll have to delay at least a day, since we still have to

186

figure out what food we're making, plus make it." He drummed his fingers on the table. "I'm really frustrated that the piroshki won't work."

He got up from the table and went over to one of the boxes. He pulled out a pillow and blanket and handed them to me. "Sleep on the floor wherever you want. I'll wake you when it's time to go."

Elias got up. "I'm going back to the town hall," he said. "I'll keep my eyes and ears open for anything that might be of use."

Birgit gathered a pillow and blankets too. "Good night," she said. "I'll be sleeping in the open cellar under the stars if you need me."

Finn laid a blanket and pillow for himself close to the hearth, and I laid mine on the other side of the room. Within minutes, we were both asleep.

I see Mama standing on the doorstep of our home in Viteretz, a smile on her face as she waves to me and Krystia walking our cow, Krasa, down the road.

I see Krasa munching on fresh grass in the pasture.

There's me and Krystia picking berries—

Raspberries . . .

Strawberries . . .

Blackberries . . .

Blueberries—

I sat up with a jolt.

I had the answer: berries.

Any kind of berries can be made into a jam. Cooled jam would hide the bitterness of the pills.

When it was time to get up the next morning, I shook Finn's shoulder. He sat up and rubbed his eyes.

"I've got the answer," I said. "Berries."

"Berries?" he replied.

"Yes, boiled with the honey, they make jam."

He thought about it for a moment, then said, "The powder would likely mix into it well. But what are you proposing, that Birgit bring a jar of jam with a spoon in the hopes of them all eating it right then and there?" He flopped back down on his pillow. "It's not going to work."

Finn had a point. Jam was the kind of thing that you ate over the course of days or weeks, not immediately.

"Pyrohy," I said.

"What are you talking about now?" said Finn with a yawn.

"Fruit pyrohy," I said. "Fried noodle on the outside, fruit jam on the inside."

Finn propped himself up to a sitting position. "That might work," he said. "Let's see what Birgit has to say."

We stepped through the corridor to the open cellar. Birgit was putting away her bedding. I told her my idea.

"That's good," she said. "We have the flour already and some fat. It's just a matter of finding berries of some sort."

"It's still spring," I said. "How do we get to the countryside from here?"

"You don't," said Birgit. "Too dangerous to try. But I might be able to find someone selling on the streets today. You and Finn can try scavenging through the destroyed buildings."

CHAPTER TWENTY-FIVE–
A HUG FROM A FRIEND
KRYSTIA

I stood there and stared at the unlatched door in confusion. Did Galina leave it unlatched on purpose? Was this some sort of elaborate trick? Or maybe it was just my good fortune that the lock didn't engage as it usually did when she banged it shut.

I longed to step out of my cell, even if just for a moment, but my feet felt glued to the floor. Would they shoot me if I stepped out?

I put my hand on the door, and with the lightest force possible, I pushed at it. The door screeched loudly as it opened a few centimeters. I held my breath. Could they hear that screeching from upstairs?

I slowly counted to one hundred, but no one opened the basement door. Maybe they hadn't heard the cell door.

I pushed it carefully once again as slowly as I could to minimize the noise. Once the opening was wide enough, I stepped through to the corridor.

My heart pounded with fear, or was it exhilaration? My heart told me to go grab the key from the hook and open Mychailo's and Sophie's doors. My head told me that this was risky and I should get back into my cell and pull the door firmly closed until the lock clicked shut.

My heart won out. I tiptoed down the corridor to the base of the stairs and retrieved the key from the hook. I had to think things through. Since Mychailo's cell was closest, it might have made sense to open his first, but if Sophie heard noises she didn't understand, she could unwittingly ask questions that could alert them, so I decided to open her cell first.

As I walked past Mychailo's cell, I showed him the key, then pointed to Sophie's cell at the end of the corridor. He nodded in understanding, then put a finger over his lips, indicating that he knew to keep silent; then he gave me a thumbs-up.

I tiptoed down to Sophie's cell. She wasn't looking out her window, and I worried that she was sleeping. I didn't want to startle her into making a sound, but I needed to do this as quickly and quietly as I could. I stuck the key into her lock and turned it. The grinding of metal on metal seemed so loud that it set my teeth on edge. I slowly and carefully pulled on Sophie's door until it was halfway open. She stood there, her eyes wide with shock. She shook her head violently, then grabbed my hair and pulled my ear close to her mouth. "This is a bad idea," she whispered.

"Let's just go unlock Mychailo and we can talk about it," I said to her in a tiny voice.

She tried to argue, but I ignored her. Maybe I was being foolish. It might have been a bad idea, but it was better than sitting in a cell and doing nothing, just waiting to be punished or killed.

Mychailo's lock was not as rusty as Sophie's, and it released without so much noise. He pushed the door open himself and he wrapped his arms around me. I could feel his body heave with sobs, so I patted his back and comforted him. Sophie surprised me by wrapping her arms around us both and sobbing as well.

If just for this one moment, I was glad that I had opened our cells. We didn't have enough food or water or heat, but this hug gave us all a new kind of strength.

I hung the key back on its hook, and Mychailo motioned for the two of us to come into his cell. Sophie and I sat side by side on his metal cot, and he sat cross-legged in front of us. Our heads were just a hair's breadth apart so we could use the faintest of whispers to talk.

"Do you think we can escape?" I asked them both.

"We can try," said Mychailo. "Although we could get killed trying."

"Staying here could also get us killed," I whispered. "The three of us are accused of working with rebel groups of various sorts. That means execution or a slave camp in Siberia."

"But I fought the Nazis," said Mychailo.

"Me too," I said.

Sophie stayed silent.

I bent as close to Mychailo's ear as I could get. "But we were fighting for freedom, not for the Soviets, and to them that's treason."

No one spoke for a minute, maybe more.

"There were others down here before you arrived," whispered Mychailo.

"What happened to them?" asked Sophie.

"The first man, I think he was executed."

"You think? Why?" I asked.

"The officer told him to remove his clothing. He was given a blanket. When he asked why, the officer said he was getting a shower. But I heard a bunch of shots—an execution squad. He never came back."

Mychailo's words made my heart pound. The Soviets' actions were just like those of the Nazis, who made their victims strip before killing them so they could reuse their clothing.

"What about the other person?" Sophie asked.

"I don't think the woman was executed. I think she was either sent to a camp or set free."

"Why do you think that?" I asked.

"The officer didn't ask for her clothing. And there were no gunshots after she left. So, we may be dead if we do nothing, and we may be dead if we do something," said Mychailo.

I nodded.

"Do either of you know how many Soviets we'd have to get through in order to escape?" whispered Sophie.

"Two guards at the entrance," I said, counting on my fingers, "and two at the door. And there are two women— the one in the embroidered blouse, but there's also one in an NKVD uniform. There's the man in the undershirt, and a man in an NKVD uniform."

"We'd have to get through eight people?" Sophie said in a whisper that was a bit too loud. "That's impossible."

"Are there still ropes tied to the interrogation chair?" asked Mychailo.

"I didn't notice," I answered.

Mychailo got up from the floor and walked to the open area. When he didn't come right back, Sophie and I went out to see what he was up to.

Mychailo was kneeling in front of the chair, and he was trying to undo one of the knots in the older frayed rope looped around one of the chair legs. "I've already untangled this," he said, holding up several loops of rope from the floor.

Sophie knelt and motioned for Mychailo to move over. She turned the chair gently on its side and slipped the ropes off. She grinned triumphantly. The knots still needed to be undone but it was easier to do that with the ropes off the chair, and if need be, we could each take some back to our cells and work on them. She handed us each a rope to work on.

We decided to do this in Sophie's cell, since it was farthest from the exit and maybe our voices wouldn't travel so easily.

"One of us can stand at the top of the stairs," whispered Mychailo. "When a person comes down, I could grab them. We could tie them up, and put them in a cell."

"And then what?" said Sophie. "They'd scream and everyone else would come down and they would shoot us."

"You're right," said Mychailo, his shoulders slumping.

"If we captured one of our captors, we'd have to gag them so they couldn't scream."

"That's true," said Sophie. "But with what?"

We looked each other up and down, trying to consider

what piece of clothing might make a good gag. I couldn't rip anything off my trousers, and if I ripped something off my shirt it would be obvious. I could tear a strip from my jacket, but it was the only thing to keep me warm. Sophie's and Mychailo's clothing had the same sort of limitations.

But—

We all wore shoes.

I was the only one without socks.

I pointed to Mychailo's and Sophie's feet. "Would either of you care to donate a sock for a good cause?" I whispered.

Sophie's face broke out into a grin. She covered her mouth with her fingers to stop from laughing out loud. Mychailo was grinning too.

"There's nothing I'd like more," he whispered, "than to shove one of my filthy, stinky socks into one of our captors' mouths."

We couldn't decide on a way to attack that wouldn't get us all killed, so in the end we each took a piece of rope to hide in our own cell, on the chance that it might come in handy. And we decided to have socks ready to use as gags. Sophie and Mychailo removed their socks, and somehow, I ended up with two dirty socks and they each got one.

"Do we leave our doors unlocked?" I asked. "Or should we lock them back up again?"

"We need to vote on it," said Sophie.

"I vote that we leave them unlocked," said Mychailo.

"Me too," I said.

Sophie didn't answer right away, but after a moment she said, "It needs to be unanimous. I vote we keep them unlocked too."

I stood up to go back to my cell but was overwhelmed with sadness. It had felt so good to have the comfort and companionship of Sophie and Mychailo, and I didn't want it to end. Sophie and Mychailo must have felt that same reluctance to the soft torture of being alone, because we all stood there, not wanting to move. Finally, I wrapped my arms around them both, relishing the freedom of being able to hug other people. "We will get out of this," I said. "And we'll escape together."

Just then, the door above the stairs opened. I grabbed my two socks and rope and scurried back to my cell. Each of us carefully, quietly eased our cell doors shut.

CHAPTER TWENTY-SIX-FOUR PYROHY
MARIA

Finn and I hunted for any kind of berries—fresh, tinned, or dried. I just needed something to work with. We methodically searched through the rubble of ruined kitchens, storehouses, root cellars, and shops, but all had been thoroughly picked over by other hungry people. Birgit told us not to go to the country, and we didn't mean to, but as we made our way through the demolished buildings on one of the side streets we somehow ended up in a treed area at the edge of town that had been either a pasture or a park at one time. A corner of the grassy spot was hidden from the road because a shed had collapsed and blocked it off. But when we checked behind it, there was an area in full sunlight and a cluster of untouched strawberry plants. Though not all the berries were ripe yet, we managed to find about thirty of varying sizes, but that wasn't enough for the filling.

"We may as well pick some of the green and white ones," I told Finn.

"Won't they be too sour?" he asked.

"Hopefully they'll sweeten up as they're cooked," I said. "But we need the volume. We've got to make do."

We stuffed our pockets and headed back. It was mid-morning by the time we got to the root cellar. Birgit was already there, looking anxious. "No one has fresh berries for barter," she said. "The only thing I could get that might work is this." She pulled a jar out of her bag that had the dregs of something red and liquid at the bottom.

I opened the jar and sniffed. A raspberry syrup or very runny jam, and not very much of it. At least it would make the strawberries go a little bit further. "This will work."

It was a challenge making the pyrohy dough and rolling it out on a table that was really a rough-surfaced door. And Finn nearly scalded himself boiling down the strawberries with the runny raspberry jam and some honey. I cut rounds of dough with the edges of a jar lid, and Finn blew on the thickened jam to cool it. We discussed with Birgit about how much of the sleeping powder should go into each pyrohy.

"We have enough jam and dough for thirty-two

pyrohy. That's four per Soviet," said Birgit. "One capsule is the recommended dose for insomnia, and anything over six is dangerous. Two should put them out."

"How many sleeping capsules do you have?" asked Finn.

"Twenty," she said.

"I say we use it all up," he said. "Some of those guards are pretty big."

We all agreed. We didn't want to kill them, just to make them go to sleep. I worried about the two women, because they were shorter and slighter than the men, but no one would have even close to a lethal dose by eating their allotted four pyrohy. Once the jam had cooled, we opened all the capsules and mixed the sleeping powder into the jam, stirring it until it dissolved. I put a spoonful of the jam/sleeping powder mixture into the middle of each raw piece of dough. Finn pinched the edges of the dough together to seal them. I boiled them lightly, then fried them crisp in fat so they wouldn't stick together in the carrying dish.

"Is Elias meeting us at the interrogation house?" I asked while placing the last pyrohy into the dish.

"No," said Finn. "It would be too suspicious if he left his police duties in the middle of the day. He'll meet us back here tonight."

I walked beside Birgit, carrying the covered dish, while Finn kept half a block behind us. The plan was for me to go in with her while Finn hid in a building across the street with his hammer and twine, waiting for the outside guards to doze off.

My stomach grumbled with hunger. Our pyrohy smelled incredibly good, and I hadn't had anything to eat since last night's dinner of bread and meat. How I wished we'd been able to find more berries. It would have been so nice if we had been able to have even just one of these delectable strawberry pyrohy each, but there had been barely enough filling for the thirty-two pyrohy as it was. Giving up such precious and tasty food was a sacrifice, but if it meant saving Krystia, Mychailo, Sophie, and others, it was well worth it.

"I hope they don't recognize me," I said to Birgit under my breath when the mansion came in sight.

"You're clean, your hair is tied back, and you're wearing different clothing. It makes you look like a local. Just don't talk and you should be fine."

One of the guards at the stone wall held his machine gun ready as he paced back and forth in front of the double-doored entrance. The second guard leaned against the wall, his eyes closed and his machine gun clasped in his arms like a baby. As we approached, the pacing guard stopped, and his eyes lit up. He lowered his gun.

"What did you bring us today, comrade?" he asked Birgit, peeking under the cloth. And then, not waiting for an answer, he grabbed one of the fruit-filled pyrohy and popped it in his mouth. "These are delicious," he said. He turned to his fellow guard. "Boris, wake up."

Boris opened his eyes. As he walked over, he looked from me to Birgit. "Who is this girl?" he asked, frowning at Birgit.

"My granddaughter, Mary," she said.

I didn't look up but kept my eyes glued on his machine gun as I held the dish out in front of me. But it was as if Boris had only half heard what Birgit said.

"Pierogi?" he asked, using the Russian word for the delicacy. "Stuffed with what? It smells delicious."

"Raspberry and strawberry," said Birgit.

"Just like Mama used to make," the guard said, brushing a tear from the corner of his eye. "How many do I get?"

"Four," said Birgit. "Not much, I know, but it was hard to find the fruit."

The guards gobbled their allotted pyrohy in less than a minute. "You should find mushrooms," said Boris. "Those are the best."

"I'll try," said Birgit as we walked through the doors and into the courtyard of the interrogation house.

The guards stationed at the bale of barbed wire

blocking the door to the mansion were just as enthusiastic about the food as the two at the gate had been. "You should have made more," said the taller of the two.

"I do my best for you," said Birgit. "Don't I bring you something special nearly every day?"

"You're better than any of the others who bring in food," said the shorter guard, biting into a pyrohy as he spoke.

We stepped past the two men as they licked the last of the jam off their fingers, and I marveled at the fact that neither of them questioned why I was with Birgit, and neither looked me in the face. But then again, why would anyone try to get into the interrogation house? The guards were mostly here to keep people from getting out.

CHAPTER
TWENTY-SEVEN–
A PRISONER
KRYSTIA

Light footsteps sounded on the stairs, and then I heard the clank of the key being taken off its hook. But as I held the bars to peek out, I inadvertently jiggled my cell door and it squeaked ever so faintly. My hands flew off the door, and the jiggling subsided. I didn't want to ruin our chance of breaking free.

Galina appeared, holding a blanket in her arms. She stepped in front of Mychailo's cell and said, "Take off your clothing. It's time for you to go."

"Where am I going?" asked Mychailo.

"For a shower," she said.

A SHOWER? I knew what that meant. Mychailo was not getting a shower, he was going to be shot. No matter how risky it was, I had no choice. I grabbed a rope and one of the stinky socks and burst out of my cell.

Galina stood there, her mouth open in surprise.

Mychailo slammed his own door open with such force that it hit her in the shoulder and she crashed to the ground. Her mouth opened wider to scream, so I sat on her stomach and shoved the dirty sock into her mouth.

She tried to pull the sock out of her mouth but I put my hand over it so she couldn't. She grabbed my hair and pulled hard. I wanted to scream, it hurt so much, but I stayed silent.

Mychailo caught both of her wrists and forced her to let go of my hair. I slid off her stomach. Sophie lunged in, helping Mychailo wrestle the woman's hands behind her back. I grabbed a rope and began wrapping it around her wrists, but Sophie took over. She was remarkably efficient with knots, and it made me wonder if Hitler Girls had taken knot-tying classes.

Galina kicked and flailed and nearly took out Mychailo's knee with the heel of her boot, so I sat on her legs and Mychailo tied her ankles together.

As all of this was unfolding, I had a sick feeling in the pit of my stomach that we were digging ourselves deeper into trouble. Soon someone from upstairs would hear the commotion and another interrogator would come down. What would we do then? We couldn't tie them all up, could we?

"Wait at the top of the steps," I said to Mychailo. "Sophie and I will get her into a cell."

As we dragged Galina into Sophie's cell, she resisted with amazing strength. I wanted to lock the door but couldn't find the key.

"It's here," said Sophie, taking it from the woman's pocket.

We slammed the cell door and locked it, just in time to hear someone else open the door at the top of the steps.

CHAPTER
TWENTY-EIGHT-
COMRADE MITKA
MARIA

When I walked into the office behind Birgit, carrying the dish of pyrohy, I noticed that only two people were at their desks, and those were the uniformed NKVD officers. My heart sank. This was not going to plan.

Birgit walked up to the woman and smiled. I was amazed at how easy it seemed for her to act as if she liked this woman. "Good day, Comrade Ludmilla," said Birgit. "I've got a special treat for you."

The woman looked up from her desk work. "What do you have today, Birgit?" she asked. "Whatever it is, it smells delicious."

Birgit took the dish from me and set it on Comrade Ludmilla's desk. With a flourish, she removed the cloth.

"I thought I smelled strawberries," said Ludmilla,

picking up a pyrohy and nibbling at the corner. "These are divine."

"There's only enough for each person to have four," said Birgit. "I wish I had been able to get more strawberries, but they're all picked over."

Comrade Ludmilla popped a second one into her mouth, and as she chewed, she slid her top drawer open. She brought out a stack of ration coupons and counted them into Birgit's hand. "No one is as good as you are in dealing with those hawkers on the black market," said the woman. "I can hardly wait to see what you concoct for us tomorrow."

"Just four each?" said the NKVD man, leaning over from his desk and grabbing a couple of pyrohy from the dish. "I could eat a dozen of these."

"Don't think you can have any of mine, Sergei," said Ludmilla, taking her own remaining two out of the dish and setting them on a cloth on her desk.

Just then, the man in the bloodied undershirt came in from the courtyard. I hadn't noticed him when we were out there. He must have been around the corner.

"It's all set for the execu—" he started to say.

"Don't you see we have guests?" said Ludmilla, pointing to us.

"Oh," he said. "Birgit, I didn't know you were here. Is this your daughter?"

He walked over to me and patted me on the head. Would he recognize me? My knees wobbled as if they were made of water, and I kept my gaze down to the floor.

"That's my granddaughter, Mary," Birgit said. "Mary, this is Mitka."

Mitka? That was a nickname for someone called Dimitri, the kind of name a mother might call a toddler. It seemed completely inappropriate for this big bully.

Mitka leaned close to the dish and sniffed. His eyes lit up. "They're filled with fruit," he said. "Just like home." He snatched three of them in his meaty hand and shoved them into his mouth.

"Just one left for you," said Birgit, handing him one more from the dish. "The other four are for Comrade Galina."

"Galina's just a scrawny thing," said Mitka, his mouth still full. "Two is all she gets. I'm starving." He grabbed two more pyrohy and gobbled them down.

I tried not to gasp. This was not going at all to plan. Mitka may have already made himself very sick by eating so much of the sleeping powder. And what of Galina? Were two pyrohy enough to make her quickly fall asleep?

I covered the last two with the cloth and grabbed the dish off the desk.

Birgit continued to chat with them as if everything were normal, but I could hardly breathe. Minutes ticked by.

Finally Birgit asked, "Where is Comrade Galina?"

"Downstairs," said Mitka. "I'll go get her."

CHAPTER TWENTY-NINE-
COMRADE GALINA
KRYSTIA

I rushed to my cell to get my second sock and another rope. I got to the base of the stairs with them just as the door at the top of the stairs opened. Mychailo's back was flat against the wall beside the door, and he held a rope in his hand.

I hid underneath the staircase.

"Galina, come upstairs," shouted the voice of the man in the bloodied undershirt. "There's a treat for you up here."

There was no answer of course. Galina thrashed around in Sophie's cell and made groaning sounds through the dirty sock stuffed in her mouth.

The top stair above me creaked. The next stair creaked.

There was a *whumph*, then a *thump, thump, thump*. I stuck my head out to see what was going on.

Mychailo had his arms around the man's chest and they were somersaulting down the stairs together. As they smashed to the bottom, I ran up the stairs and eased the door nearly shut, but didn't let the lock engage. I didn't want the people up there to be able to hear what was going on, but I didn't want the door to close and lock us in either.

I rushed down the stairs to help Mychailo, but strangely he needed no help. The man in the bloodied undershirt was splayed out on the floor, his muscles loose, and a string of drool hanging from the corner of his lip.

"Did you kill him?" I whispered to Mychailo.

"I barely touched him," said Mychailo. "It's like he fell asleep halfway down the staircase."

Sophie knelt beside the man and put her finger under his nose. "He's breathing." She rolled him onto his side, and we tied his hands behind his back.

I bent to tie his feet, but Sophie shook her head. "He's out," she said. "Save the rope. We may need it."

Mychailo dragged him while Sophie and I pushed. It was like trying to move a dead cow, but we finally got him into my cell.

"What should we do now?" I whispered.

"They'll check on him soon," said Mychailo, tucking

a length of rope into his back pocket. "We need to be ready."

Mychailo positioned himself at the top of the stairs again, while Sophie and I crouched side by side beneath the staircase, barely daring to breathe.

CHAPTER THIRTY– THE BASEMENT
MARIA

Birgit stood in front of Ludmilla's desk while I stood slightly behind her, the dish with the last two pyrohy clutched to my chest. I was amazed by how relaxed and friendly Birgit could act with Ludmilla, chatting about the weather and food and ingredients and what was and wasn't available to buy on the black market (as long as you had the money or coupons).

I was glad she could do it, because Ludmilla didn't seem to be aware of what Mitka was doing in the basement. What *was* he doing? Had he fallen down the stairs? That's what it sounded like, and it was entirely possible, seeing as he'd eaten an awful lot of that sleeping powder. But why hadn't Galina come up yet?

Sergei yawned. He kept on tapping away on his

typewriter, but the tempo had slowed and seemed staggered. Ludmilla didn't seem tired at all.

I wondered about the guards outside. If they were asleep, Finn might come in here at any time, but if these two NKVD agents weren't asleep, that would be a problem. And what if Galina came up just at that time? Even one of those things would ruin our plan.

I tugged on Birgit's sleeve, and she looked over to me. I jerked my head toward the door. Maybe we could head off Finn.

"You've got work to do," said Birgit, edging away from the desk. "I'll see you tomorrow, hopefully with something tasty."

"Have a good day," said Ludmilla. She lifted her hand to wave, but then her eyes fluttered shut, and her head smacked onto her desk.

I looked over to Sergei. He was out too, sprawled back on his chair, with his arms hanging limp at his sides.

At that moment, Finn appeared breathless at the door. "All four guards are asleep," he said. "I dragged the two at the wall into the courtyard so they wouldn't raise suspicion, and I've tied their hands."

I jerked my head over to the two sleeping NKVD agents. "They just fell asleep," I said. "And Mitka, the man in the undershirt, ate more than his share, and I think I heard him fall down the basement stairs."

"What about the other woman?" asked Finn.

"Mitka was going down to get her," I said. "I have no idea why she hasn't come up."

"Do you think she's figured out what we're doing up here?" he whispered.

"We need to go down there and find out," I said.

Birgit stepped behind Ludmilla's desk. She opened a drawer and pulled out a thick stack of ration coupons. She stuffed them in a pocket and opened another drawer. "I'm looking for her pistol," she said.

"I'll go down there," I said. "But I'm not taking a pistol."

"Galina could kill you," said Birgit.

"If she sees me with a gun, she'll shoot for sure," I said.

"Take the hammer," said Finn, drawing it out of his pocket and handing it to me.

I wasn't happy with the thought of attacking someone with a hammer, but I took it just in case. It was more useful than nothing and better than a gun. I set the remaining pyrohy on one of the desks and ran to the cellar door. I pulled it open and stepped inside.

CHAPTER THIRTY-ONE-
TOGETHER
KRYSTIA

The door opened, followed by a few moments of menacing silence. Suddenly there was a *whumph*, then grunting and struggles, and a cry. A hammer clattered to the basement floor. I jumped away and missed being struck by mere centimeters.

"Let me *go!*" cried the voice. A very familiar voice!

"Maria?" I whisper-shouted.

"Krystia! Help me!"

I heard more grunts and struggling on the stairs. "Mychailo," I whispered. "Let her go. That's my sister."

A woman's silhouette appeared at the top of the stairs. "Mychailo? Is that you?"

"Baba!" cried Mychailo. He ran up the stairs and hugged the woman.

Maria flew down the stairs and we nearly collided. I wrapped my arms around her. We hugged and wept.

"Thank goodness you're safe," she said, but then she untangled herself from me. "We have to hurry. Where is Galina? She could come for us at any moment!"

I nearly laughed out loud as I grabbed my sister's hand. "Come here and I'll show you," I said, tugging her toward the last cell. I opened the door. Galina struggled, her eyes wild. As we watched, she finally spit out the filthy sock and screamed, "Let me out!"

"Shout all you want," said Maria. "Your friends are sound asleep."

Sophie appeared beside us, a length of rope lashed around one fist and a dirty sock in the other. She looked at Maria and said, "What do we need to do now?"

"The other prisoners in this place," said Maria. "We need to rescue them." She turned and ran up the stairs. I picked up the hammer from the floor, then Sophie and I followed close behind.

We burst out into the kitchen and ran to the main office room. The first thing I noticed was the delectable aroma of strawberries. There was a dish sitting there, covered by a cloth. I moved the cloth and spied two crispy pyrohy, strawberry jam oozing out of them.

I grabbed one and was about to cram it in my mouth

when Maria snatched it out of my hand and put it back in the dish. "Don't eat that," she shouted. "It's got sleeping powder in it."

And now I understood. My brilliant little sister and her friends had pulled off a coup. I saw the two sleeping NKVD officers at their desks. I ran to the front door and saw the guards both slumped on the ground, fast asleep. And over by the stone wall there were two other sleeping guards.

Mychailo and the older woman were rooting through the desk drawers. "That's Birgit," Maria said, gesturing toward the woman. "Mychailo's grandmother."

I nodded to her, and she smiled at me. I recognized her as the woman who brought us food and gave us her blessing.

"This should help!" said Mychailo, holding up a large ring with maybe a dozen keys on it. "Krystia, catch."

I reached my hand up and caught the keys as they flew toward me. "I'm starting on the top floor," I said. I had hopes of taking the steps two at a time, but with all this excitement, plus the lack of food, I was woozy and weak. I clutched the banister as Finn stepped in beside me. He gently took the keys out of my hand.

"Can you tie the interrogators' hands?" he asked, handing me a ball of twine and taking the hammer from me.

"I can do that," I said.

"Great," said Finn. Then he ran up the stairs. Maria was right behind him.

"After you tie the interrogators' hands, can you help us look through the desks?" asked Mychailo.

"What are you looking for?" I asked.

"Our papers," he said. "It will be so much easier to escape if we can find them. Also, cash and ration coupons."

CHAPTER THIRTY-TWO–
"VICHNAYA PAMYAT"
MARIA

Since we had no idea how long we had before the guards and interrogators woke up, there was no time to waste. We had to release the other prisoners in this horrible place.

It was nerve-racking going from interrogation room to interrogation room, starting with the third floor. At first, I couldn't make out the order of the keys on the big iron ring, but after a few false tries I realized that they were color-coded. Keys marked with blue paint were the top floor, red was for the second floor, unmarked for the main floor, and black for the basement.

On the third floor we found just one person—in the room that was beside mine. A man, nearly unconscious, tied to a chair. Once I loosened the knots for him, he had to lean on both Finn and me to get down the stairs.

Krystia took him into the kitchen and got him water while Finn and I ran back up the stairs to the second floor.

There were four interrogation rooms on this level. All were empty except for one, but the teenaged boy tied to the chair in that room was dead. My heart ached at the sight of him, and I wondered about his parents, his family, people who would never see him again. I longed to have the time to sing the "Vichnaya Pamyat" for his soul, but we could not spare it, so I settled on covering his face with a small cloth that I found in one of the rooms, then saying a short prayer.

On the main floor, there was the cell where Finn had been imprisoned for a short while, but it was now empty. The only other one was the big holding room where we all had initially been imprisoned.

We opened it up and found four girls our age, two older boys, plus an elderly man and woman. At first, they all cowered and cringed together in the far corner, but Finn held the door wide open and I said, "We were captives too. We're here to help you escape."

They rushed out of the room, shaking our hands and hugging each other for joy.

"How long have you been here?" Finn asked one of the boys.

"A couple of us were brought in yesterday. The others got here today."

"From where?" asked Finn.

"Me? The British zone. The Soviets came into our refugee camp and selected us. The Brits didn't interfere, even though we told them we were not Soviet citizens."

The group headed to the mansion entrance, but I called to them, "Please, stay a little while and help us."

"What would you like us to do?" asked the older woman.

"Look out to the courtyard," I said, pointing to the two sleeping guards just outside the door as well as the two slumped on the ground near the stone wall, their hands bound with twine. "We need to buy ourselves some time. That means locking all four of the guards into cells."

"That's a very good idea," said the woman. She motioned to the girls and pointed to the guards at the door. "Help me drag these ones in."

The girls were bone-thin and the woman walked with a limp, but they got to work and dragged in the first guard.

"Who will help me get those guards in?" said the man, pointing to the guards near the wall.

The two boys went out with him and got to work.

Once all four guards were in the big cell on the main

floor, I found a pot in the kitchen and filled it with water. Finn helped me carry it to the cell, but as we set it down, he said, "These guards didn't care enough to bring any of us water."

"They didn't ask to be Soviet guards," I said. "And we have no idea how long it will take for them to be found. Besides, they'll be really thirsty when they wake up."

I filled another container with water and set it in the other cell on the main floor, and then Finn and I dragged in Sergei and Ludmilla.

"We have to get out of here as soon as we can," said Birgit. "Soviet soldiers could come at any time with a new group of prisoners."

"You're right," I said. "But there's one more thing that I need to do."

I carried two cups of water down to the basement. I unlocked Mitka's cell to check on him. He was still deeply asleep, so I untied his hands and left one of the cups of water on his cot before locking it back up.

When I opened Galina's cell, she tried to kick me with her bound feet. "You will pay for this," she said in a voice hoarse from screaming. "I will track you all down and kill you myself."

I knelt close to her head and held a cup of water to her lips. "Drink some of this now," I said.

She turned her head away.

"You have no idea how long you're going to be down here," I said.

"Then you should let me go."

"Just drink."

She took a few sips and swallowed them down. I placed the cup on her cot.

"I can't drink that if I'm tied up and you know it," she sputtered.

"I'm sure you'll wiggle out of those ropes in no time," a voice behind me said.

It was Krystia. My sister stood at the door of the cell, holding a plate. "This is in case you get hungry," she said, placing the plate on the cot beside the water.

On the plate were the last two drugged fruit pyrohy.

I locked the cell door. Krystia and I went up the stairs.

"Are you ready to go now?" asked Birgit, her eyes wide with anxiety.

"Yes," I said, looking around. Krystia stood beside me, and Finn was there as well. Birgit and Mychailo too. "Where's Sophie?"

"She left a while ago," said Mychailo. "As soon as we found the papers identifying her as Bianka Holata, she grabbed them from me, plus she took a stack of ration coupons and was out the door."

Was I surprised that she left without even a thank-you or goodbye? Not really. It just proved that the Hitler Girl hadn't changed her ways. But dare I admit to being a little bit disappointed? Deep in my heart I had hoped she had changed. And I had made her a new outfit. Now I wouldn't even be able to give it to her. I could feel tears well up in my eyes. I brushed my face with the back of my hand.

"Forget about her," said Krystia, wrapping her arm around my shoulders. "Let's just hope she can look after herself."

Krystia, Finn, Mychailo, Birgit, and I walked out of the interrogation house. But were we free?

CHAPTER THIRTY-THREE– THURINGIA
KRYSTIA

I barely remembered weaving our way through the war-ravaged city streets, my hand clasped in Maria's. When we dropped down into the hidden root cellar, at first I felt claustrophobic. I had been locked up for days, and what I wanted most right then was to feel the sun on my face and the wind on my back.

"Come this way," said Maria. She led me to a second room that had no ceiling. I lay down on the dirt floor and stared up at the sky, and for the first time in a long time, I felt free.

Maria came back a few minutes later with a stack of clothing, a bar of soap, and some rags. She set the clothing on my lap. "I made this for you."

It was a blue dress and pink blouse just like what she

wore. I was so overwhelmed that I could not speak. Maria helped me wash away the grime and the dust and the blood, and she poured soapy water through my hair. As the layers of dirt sloughed off me, I felt like the hurt was washing away as well. When I put on the new clothing, I felt like I was reborn.

"One more thing," said Maria, holding something behind her back.

"What do you have?" I asked.

She held out the item she had been hiding: a bright red pair of homemade underpants.

"These are quite bright." I held them up to my waist and could tell that she had sized them perfectly.

Maria smiled. "I made them from a Nazi flag."

That made me giggle. I couldn't think of a more perfect use for all those flags that were suddenly hidden all over Germany. I slipped them on, then gave Maria a big hug. I could have curled up in a ball and slept forever, I was that exhausted, but Maria said, "Not now. Elias is back."

I nearly had a heart attack when I saw Elias in his Soviet police jacket.

"Have you gone to the other side?" I asked him.

He walked over to me, and I noticed that his limp was more pronounced than before. "I wasn't a Nazi when the Germans forced me to wear their uniform, and I'm certainly no Soviet now. I agreed to work with them so that Finn and I would be released."

He opened his arms to give me a hug, but I stepped away.

"Are you still working with them?" I asked.

"They think I am," he said. "And that's good news for us." He took the jacket off and threw it to the ground. He pulled a folded paper out of his trousers pocket. "I've been able to find out a lot of information about where the Soviet zone ends and how to get to the closest American border. I've created a map that should get us out of here." He opened it up and spread it out on the table.

Some light filtered through the broken ceiling, but it was not enough to see the fine printing on the map, so Birgit lit a candle and set it on the table. Elias smoothed out the map and we all crowded around.

"This is where we came from," he said, pointing to Karlsfeld, close to Munich. "And this is where we are now." He pointed to a spot that didn't even have a name, but it was about halfway between Berlin and Dresden.

"We traveled hundreds of kilometers in that truck?" I asked.

"We did," said Elias. "And as you can see from this map, we're right in the middle of what is officially the Soviet zone."

I studied the map. Germany was sectioned off into

French, British, American, and Soviet occupation zones. A hundred kilometers or more to the northwest of us, the Soviets shared a border with the British zone and about four hundred kilometers to the southwest of us, the Soviets shared a border with the American zone.

"There's no way that we can get back to the Americans," I said. "Even to get to the British means walking through the Soviet zone for days, maybe even weeks. And we'll be hunted down as soon as the interrogators wake up."

"You would be right," said Elias with a smile. "Except the Americans currently occupy a big chunk of the Soviet zone." He took his pencil and shaded over most of the province of Thuringia and he put an X on a spot close to where we were.

"What's that place?" I asked.

"This is the closest place where the Americans currently are," he said, tapping the pencil. "This is Torgau."

"How many kilometers is that from us?" I asked.

"About twenty," he said.

"Twenty kilometers? That's all?" I asked. My eyes filled with tears. I clasped Maria around the waist. I felt like dancing.

"Hold on," said Elias. "Just because it's close doesn't mean it's easy. The area between us and them is officially a forbidden zone for travel."

"This is farmland and forest," said Birgit, moving her fingers over the area on the map between us and the Americans. "I know some of these people because I've lived in this town my whole life. They're good and kind folk."

"The Americans have blocked all the main roads going into the American zone from the east," said Elias. "But that's mostly to keep out German soldiers. The Americans have also blocked off footpaths and smaller roads to keep people out. They're trying to channel refugees who want to enter the American zone in through the few main roads that they've marked as official frontier crossing points so they can check everyone out before they're let in."

"So once we get into the farmland and forest area it shouldn't be as difficult," I said. "The hardest part will be to get out of the Soviet zone, correct?"

"It's going to be tricky," said Elias. "And timing is critical."

"Because the interrogators will be hunting us down?" I asked.

"That's just half the problem," said Elias. "This entire area"—he swept his fingers over the part of the map that he grayed out with the pencil—"is supposed to be Soviet but it's currently occupied by the Americans. But it's scheduled to be handed over to the Soviets very soon."

"Do you know when?" I asked.

"The exact date is a secret, but rumors say it will be in the first week of July."

And I realized that I had no concept of time. In late May we had entered the American refugee camp. How many days . . . or weeks had passed since then?

"What is today's date?" I asked.

"It's June twenty-eighth," he said.

"Twenty kilometers isn't that far," I said.

"We need to get to the Americans in about two days, then," said Finn. "Or the border will move away from us and we'll be in big trouble."

"Once we get out of the Soviet zone it shouldn't be bad," said Birgit. "But we can't go as a group. I have decided that Mychailo and I will go first thing tomorrow morning. Mychailo needs to get in one good meal and a few hours' sleep before the long trek."

I barely knew Mychailo, but spending that time with him in the downstairs prison bound him to me in a way I could barely put into words. I didn't want him and Birgit traveling on their own. "Wouldn't we be safer in a group?"

"Think about it," said Birgit. "The interrogators know me better than all of you combined, and they'd consider me as the instigator of the breakout. They'll be hunting me down."

Birgit did have a point, but I didn't agree with her

solution. "But if we travel in a group, we're less likely to get lost, and we can watch out for each other."

"We can watch out for you better if we go before you," said Mychailo. "Baba"—he nodded at his grandma—"knows the farmers who live between here and Torgau."

"That's right," said Birgit. "Some will help us out of friendship, others if we give them ration coupons or cash. But we can tell them that you will be coming next, and we can ask them to assist you."

"Getting through the Soviet checkpoint on the outskirts of town is our biggest obstacle," said Mychailo. "Baba has papers identifying her as a local and she's allowed out to buy supplies. As long as the interrogators haven't been freed yet and no one's been notified about her, she should be able to walk out of the checkpoint."

"But what about you, Mychailo?" I asked.

"I'll have to figure it out as I go. We'll all be figuring it out as we go."

"I agree that Birgit and Mychailo should escape together," said Elias. "Finn and I will be going on our own as well."

Maria sighed deeply. "I felt like we were a family. A team. But now we're getting all split up again."

"Birgit is a target," said Elias. "But I've deserted my position as a Soviet policeman to go to the West. They'd consider that treason."

"We have only one map," I said.

"None of us are taking this with us," said Elias. "You'll have to memorize it. Do you know what the Soviets would do to you if they caught you with a map like this?"

"Good point," I said. "How should we stagger our departure?"

"Finn and I leave tonight," said Elias. "We've had the most time to recuperate from being in the interrogation house, so we'll carve the way."

"But Birgit knows the farmers in the forbidden zone," I said. "You don't."

"We're German," said Finn. "So are the farmers. They'll help us." He smiled. "And we'll tell them we know Birgit."

"One last meal together before you go," said Birgit. "And hopefully we'll see you all on the other side."

CHAPTER THIRTY-FOUR–
LAST FEAST
MARIA

We still had flour, fat and honey, two carrots, plus a tin of meat, so before Finn and Elias left, we had a feast. We boiled rainwater so we'd have something to drink, and as it cooled, I insisted that both Krystia and Mychailo rest while Finn, Elias, Birgit, and I made a big batch of noodles to use up every last bit of the flour. We boiled the noodles, then fried them in the fat. I set the honey out on a dish in the middle of the table, and we dipped the fresh crispy noodles into it.

"These are heavenly," said Krystia, her eyes closed and her face looking like she was in a trance as she savored her crispy honeyed noodles one bite at a time.

We sliced the carrots and made sure each of us had equal portions, and then we passed the spoon and tin of meat around, and each of us enjoyed a mouthful of meat as well. We also drank down every last bit of the boiled rainwater.

When all the food and water was gone, Elias put his Soviet police jacket back on.

"Shouldn't you leave that here?" I asked. "If you're caught in that while you're escaping, you said yourself that they might shoot you."

"It's a good cover for now, and it will help us get through town," said Elias. "Who knows? It might even help me get through the checkpoint. I'll ditch it once we're in the countryside."

"Take this," said Birgit, pressing a stack of ration coupons and Soviet cash into Elias's and Finn's hands.

I was filled with sadness as I watched them leave. At the last minute, Finn turned, and he gave me a fierce hug. "I'm really going to miss you," he said.

"Me too," I replied.

Elias held out his hand. I took it in mine and gave it a firm shake.

"Until the other side," he said.

And then they were gone.

The four of us remaining went back to the main root cellar and pored over the map. "Keep the roads in your sight, but try to avoid the other refugees," said Birgit.

"Especially in the first kilometer or so, when there could be Soviet border guards patrolling the area."

"That's good advice," I said. "Thank you." I put my hand on her forearm and said, "Now I'm going to give you some advice."

Birgit's eyebrows rose. "Oh?"

"Wear that scarf and coat that you used to disguise yourself when you found me outside the interrogation house," I said. "If the interrogators have been freed, your description will be circulated."

Birgit smiled. "I can do much better than that." With a flourish she removed the kerchief and shook out her thick curly brown hair. "Do I look different now?" she asked.

"For some reason I always thought you had gray hair," I said.

"I also have a different colored dress and jacket," she said. "Different from what I always wore at the interrogation house, and different from what I wore when I found you freed."

"It sounds like you've thought of everything," I said.

"Not quite everything," said Birgit. "If they recognize my name on my identity papers I'll still be in trouble."

"Let's hope it doesn't come to that." I turned to Mychailo. "How are you going to change your appearance?"

"Elias found a shirt and cap for me," said Mychailo.

237

"With that, and getting a good wash with soap and water before I go to sleep tonight, I should blend in with the locals."

Mychailo reached into his pocket and handed me some Soviet cash and ration coupons. He handed Krystia her refugee papers. "In case we don't see you before we leave tomorrow morning," he said.

Birgit set the ration coupons and cash from her own pockets onto the table. "We'll divide the rest of this into four equal portions," she said. "That way we'll be all set for tomorrow."

After we counted it all out and tucked it away, Birgit patted my hand and said, "We'll leave just before sunrise tomorrow morning. Give us an hour, and then you and Krystia should leave. We'll pave the way for you as best we can."

"Thank you," I said, giving her a fierce hug. "We would never have gotten out of the interrogation house without your help."

"We're a good team," said Birgit, patting my back. "Now let's all get some sleep so we're ready for our journey."

I knew that Krystia would have preferred to sleep under the stars, but Mychailo still needed the privacy to wash, so we dragged some of the blankets and bedding close to the hearth in the main room and nestled in.

"We did it," whispered Krystia, snuggling in beside me, wrapping her arms around my waist. Her face shone like a pearl in the bits of moonlight that filtered through the ceiling, and for a moment she looked like Mama.

"Not quite," I said. "A lot can go wrong between here and the American zone. We've got to be careful."

"Don't worry," said Krystia. "I'll protect you." And she squeezed my hand.

Her words stunned me. I knew they were said out of love. And when we were little, she did protect me. But now? We both protected each other. A surge of anger and frustration rippled through my stomach and I pulled my hand away from hers.

"What's the matter?" she asked.

"You've often put us at more risk," I said. "Because sometimes you act before thinking."

"You don't understand," said Krystia. "Sometimes it takes a bold action to turn things around."

"Like hiding under the cots in the barrack?" I said. "Or refusing to get in the truck, and almost getting me shot?"

"That's not fair," said Krystia. "We wouldn't have been found if Sophie hadn't ratted us out. I was only trying to protect you."

"Just like you protected Mama?"

Krystia went still.

I would have taken the words back if I could, but the damage was done.

Tears welled up in Krystia's eyes. "You think I got Mama killed?"

"No," I said. "I'm sorry. The words fell out of my mouth."

Krystia pushed away from me and stood up. "You have no idea how hard it was after you abandoned us to run away with Nathan."

My heart caught in my throat. "Abandoned you?" I said. "I left to make it easier on you and Mama. Only two mouths to feed instead of three. And I thought I could send money home. Besides, I had to save Nathan."

"It wasn't easier," said Krystia, pacing. "It was like carrying the weight of the world on my shoulders. How I would have loved to be able to just run away to a quiet farm like you had."

"But maybe if you had run away, and helped Mama to run away, she'd still be alive," I said.

Krystia stopped pacing. She looked at me, and her eyes no longer welled with tears. Now they flashed with anger. "You make it sound like Mama was passive. Like I could have ever told her what to do. How could you think that our mama was anything but brave and fierce? She knew the risks we were taking to hide Dolik, Leon, and Mr. Segal from the killing squads. She and I both decided that we had to take the chance, even if we both died trying."

I couldn't say anything to that because my heart was so filled with sorrow. Yes, Mama had always been headstrong, much like Krystia. She did brave and stupid things like my sister too. I was so proud and angry with her. And I was proud and angry with my sister. None of my friends' mothers would dig a hole in their kitchen floor to hide their friends from the Nazis. None of my friends' mothers would ever dream of hiding an entire slaughtered cow from the Nazis. Mama's stupid, headstrong bravery was legendary. It had always been me who was the careful one of us three. And running off with Nathan so we could hide in plain sight was the bravest and stupidest thing I had ever done.

And then my heart nearly stopped beating because I had a horrible thought.

"Krystia," I said. "Maybe if I had been at home, I could have saved Mama."

Krystia stopped pacing. "No one told Mama what to do. She was her own person."

"I know that," I said. "But maybe she needed me

around to make her think twice. I'm sorry for blaming you for Mama's death."

Krystia came back to me then. "I forgive you for saying that. We've both been grieving." She knelt beside me and wrapped her arms around my shoulders. "Maria, Mama was so proud of what you did. And of all of us, you were the one who succeeded."

"She was proud of me?" I was overwhelmed with tears.

"She was in awe," said Krystia, her voice catching. "And so am I." The words were like a balm to my soul.

"You don't think I'm timid?"

I could feel Krystia's shoulders shaking, and for a moment I thought she was weeping, but then I realized that she was giggling.

"You haven't been timid for a very long time," she replied. "But you are more careful than I am, and don't you think that makes us a good team?"

"We could be a good team," I said. "But I need you to promise me something."

"What?" she asked.

"Stop treating me like your little sister."

Krystia tilted her head. "Keeping you safe is the most important thing in my life."

"I want to keep you safe too. Which means sometimes

you've got to listen to me and take my advice. I am the careful one, after all."

She took in a deep breath and then exhaled slowly. A small smile formed on her lips. "Okay. No big sister and little sister. We're equal sisters."

CHAPTER THIRTY-FIVE– CHECKPOINT
KRYSTIA

Early the next morning, Maria and I blended in with the scavengers, as if we were locals. She carried a tin pail and we each dropped things into it from time to time as we slowly made our way toward the checkpoint on the western side of the town. When we finally got there, Maria dumped the items out of her bucket when no one was looking.

The Soviet zone ended at the checkpoint where the main road exited town. My sister and I walked on the main road toward the checkpoint and pretended that it was the most natural thing in the world to do—just two local girls out picking berries. Our plan worked until we were about two blocks away from the checkpoint when a German in a Soviet police jacket stepped in front of us. "Where do you think you're going?" he asked.

Maria held up her pail and looked at him with wide eyes. "We're not having much luck scavenging today, so we thought we'd try picking berries in the country," she said, pointing toward the checkpoint.

"Not many berries left for picking," he replied. "And I doubt they'll let you out for that. It's dangerous out in the country, you know."

"Maybe," said Maria. "But we don't have anything to eat. Could we just ask the border guards?"

He looked us over. We had no supplies with us, not even jackets.

He shrugged. "Go ahead and try."

I gave him a big smile and grabbed my sister's hand. When we got to the checkpoint, it was clogged with a long line of refugees waiting to get through. We stood off to one side to watch. The guards spent several minutes poring over each person's papers one by one, and very few people were allowed to go through.

"This isn't going to work," Maria said as she tugged me behind a heaved-up concrete boulder. "If there wasn't a lineup we could have approached them, but it would be suspicious for us to stand for hours in that lineup all on the pretense of wanting to collect berries."

"You're right," I said. "Maybe we should show them our papers and hope for the best."

"We don't have the right papers though," said Maria.

"What do you mean?" I asked, pulling my papers out of my pocket. "You were given yours, and we found mine in the desks, remember?" I flipped mine to the last page, the one where the letter from the Americans was attached, acknowledging that I was a displaced person under the protection of the American zone.

"There," I said, stabbing my finger at the American letter. "That's our ticket out."

"No, it isn't," she said. "We're supposed to be locals, out picking berries. If we were locals, we'd have Soviet papers that identified us as locals."

"Good point," I said, my stomach feeling queasy. "I guess our papers will only become useful once we're trying to reenter the American zone."

What I didn't say out loud was that I hoped the Soviets didn't find these papers on us because having refugee papers from the American zone was like waving a red flag to get their attention. The only way we would be here with papers like ours was if we were captured by the Soviets and brought here—as criminals. All the more reason not to wait in the lineup.

"Did you see what else my papers say?" Maria pulled out her own papers and showed me what was typed in Russian on the back.

"What does that say?" I asked.

"It's my instructions to report to mandatory slave labor. This is worse than no documents."

"We need to sneak through, then," I said.

"Mychailo would have had the same trouble. Finn too," said Maria. "I wonder how they got through."

"Maybe they didn't," I said.

Maria sighed, then sat down on a hunk of concrete. "Twenty kilometers never seemed so far away," she said.

"Let's watch the guards," I said. "To see their pattern."

We slipped back out from behind the concrete slab and pretended to scavenge but kept a close eye on the border guards. There were still just the two of them like when we were brought here by force, but that was two guards too many. This town was on a hill, and from their vantage point, they had a wide view of the road leading up to it and the surrounding countryside. They had a good view for quite a distance. This meant that even if we managed to find another way to get out of town, they'd still see us.

As we pretended not to watch them, the lineup thinned out, and for a while there was no one waiting. Just then, a scene unfolded in front of me that made my heart stand still.

Sophie approached the gate.

I elbowed Maria.

247

As we watched, Sophie strode up to the border guards and showed them her papers. She didn't use any sort of ploy at all. "Why would she think they would let her out?" I whispered to Maria.

"You would have tried the same thing if I hadn't stopped you," said Maria. "You thought our American letter was our ticket out of here."

She had a point. "Let's see what happens," I said.

As we watched Sophie make her fatal mistake, I felt so sad. If only she had stayed with us we might have been able to help her. The guards blocked the gate so she couldn't step through. She pulled out a stack of ration coupons and tried to stuff them in the hands of one of the guards, but that only made him angry. He yelled at her, and the coupons fluttered onto the ground.

A crowd gathered around Sophie and the guards. Some seemed content just to listen and find out what would happen to her, but others had their eyes locked on the coupons that were fluttering in the breeze. None of them risked grabbing one while the guards were there, but perhaps they were waiting for their chance when a guard turned his back.

One guard shook his fist at Sophie while the other spoke to someone over a field radio. Sophie sat down on a concrete block and held her head in her hands. It looked like she was weeping. That German in the Soviet police jacket appeared. He handcuffed Sophie and took her away.

My heart broke for Sophie. Much as I despised her, I hated to see her in trouble. Also, her trouble could soon be ours if we couldn't figure out a way to get through the checkpoint. Would she end up back at the interrogation house? Or maybe worse, a Soviet camp? Or execution?

If she ended up back in the interrogation house, she'd inform on us for sure. We needed to get out.

An hour passed, maybe more. The guards didn't take a break. A group was herded at gunpoint up to the gate from the forbidden zone. It felt like I was watching what happened to us not long ago. The guards chatted with the Red Army soldiers, and then the whole sorry group was forced through the barricade. As they passed, they walked so close that I could almost feel their sorrow.

"We've got to take a chance," I said to Maria. "We're wasting the whole day."

I began to walk toward the guards, but Maria caught my arm. "They could arrest us again," she said. "They'll throw us back into the interrogation house, and that will be the death of us."

Just then, a boy about our age approached us. "Is one of you Maria?" he asked.

My sister nodded. "And what's your name?" he asked me.

"Krystia," I said.

He smiled. "Good," he said. "You're friends of Birgit. She told me to watch for you. Follow me."

He took us to a tumbledown building near the checkpoint, and we climbed the stairs to a room on the second story. It was a miracle that the floor hadn't collapsed, but other than not having one of its walls, the room looked uncannily domestic. "Sit," he said, gesturing toward a dusty sofa.

We sat.

He grabbed a stool and sat in front of us.

"You're trying to get to the American zone?" he asked.

"Yes," I said.

"Birgit said you can pay me."

"We can," I said. "Do you prefer Soviet cash or ration coupons?"

"I prefer American cash," he said with a grin, "but I'll take ration coupons. You know the short guard? The one with the gray hair? You can bribe him with ration coupons to let you through."

"How much?" I asked.

"Three ration cards each should do it," he said. "And the same for me for my trouble."

"Thank you."

"Okay," he said. "Let's go down there to wait. The tall one goes on break any time now."

CHAPTER THIRTY-SIX–
FORBIDDEN ZONE
MARIA

I watched the boy and the short guard exchange the ration coupons and chat about the weather. The guard turned to us and said, "What are you waiting for? Run! My partner will be back in fifteen minutes."

The road was downhill, which was a blessing. Krystia and I took off as fast as we could, sprinting down the hill. After fifteen minutes of running, I was gasping for air, but when I turned and looked at the checkpoint, I could see that we were still in full view.

"This way," said Krystia, darting behind a cluster of overgrown weeds. We dashed from one bush or rock to another until the checkpoint was finally out of view.

I bent over almost double, heaving for air and nearly vomiting. After we caught our breath, we walked and walked and walked some more. Through meadows with grass that went to our hips and climbing up stony hills that crumbled below our shoes with every step. We walked past fields that hadn't been sown this spring and waded through icy-cold creeks and slimy swamps. We did see other refugees from time to time, but we kept away from them.

We walked all day and all through the night, and we only rested twice. Once, as we walked through a bomb-blasted cow pasture, a woman came out from the farmhouse to greet us. "Are you Birgit's friends?" she asked.

"We are," I said.

"You need to tell me your names," said the woman. "Anyone can say they know Birgit."

"I'm Maria, and this is Krystia. We're sisters," I said.

"Good," she said. "Come into the house. I'll give you a meal."

Her kitchen had a flagstone floor and there were bundles of garlic hanging from the rafters. She poured us each a big glass of milk and gave us each a thick slice of rye bread slathered with fresh butter.

"Can we give you ration coupons for this?" I asked, pulling some out of my pocket and setting them on the table.

"Put them back, child. You may need them for someone

else. Birgit told me what you've been through, and I'm not about to take payment from you."

"Thank you," said Krystia.

"You are so kind," I said.

As I ate that bread and drank that milk, it did more than just fill up my stomach. It gave me hope for the future, for the common decency of regular people. This woman had suffered in the war too. That I knew. And she had also been propagandized into thinking that people like me and Krystia weren't even human, yet she welcomed us into her house and shared with us what little she had.

When we were finished, she walked out with us and pointed into the distance. "Walk, keeping the ruined railway tracks on your left side for about five kilometers," she said. "You'll see a barn with a red roof. That farmer will help you next."

CHAPTER THIRTY-SEVEN– AMERICAN ZONE
KRYSTIA

From the distance it looked like a black line of charcoal on a landscape painting, but when we got closer, I saw that it was a vast barricade of trucks and tanks and barbed wire bales. American flags flapped high in the wind.

"We should go onto the main road now," said Maria. "I'm done with sneaking."

I agreed with her, partly because I was utterly exhausted and wanted to get this last leg of our journey completed, but also because as we got closer, all but the main road was blocked.

We followed the arrows on the hand-painted signs that directed us to the nearest frontier crossing point, and we took our place amid the hundreds of others who were also waiting to cross into the American zone.

There were desks set up and harried officers sitting at them, screening each person one by one. Not everyone was let through. This was like a dream—or nightmare—on repeat. It was just like what we did at the end of the war.

I clutched my papers, hoping that the Americans wouldn't find a reason to deny us help.

"Come forward," said an older soldier with tired-looking eyes. Maria and I stepped in front of his table together.

I opened my papers and spread them out. Maria did the same with hers.

"You've already got this," he said in German, shaking the letter from the Americans in Karlsfeld recognizing me as a refugee. "Why were you galivanting all over the forbidden zone? You should have stayed in the American camp in Karlsfeld."

His words made me angry. Didn't he realize that my fondest dream was to stay in the American camp in Karlsfeld? We had thought we were safe there. I felt like shouting and shaking my fist, but I knew that wouldn't help. I took a deep breath and stayed calm.

"The Soviets kidnapped us," I said. "We escaped and walked back to the American zone."

The soldier sighed with impatience. "Turn around, both of you, slowly, with your hands up," he said.

My heart sank. Was he turning us away?

"Okay," he said. "You're obviously not smugglers. You've got nothing on you, not even jackets. But how do I know that you're telling the truth?"

"Do you read Russian?" asked Maria.

"A little," he said.

"Look at this." She flipped her American letter and showed the Russian text, where she was ordered for hard labor and then deportation. "We were captured," she said. "And tortured. But we escaped."

"I've heard this story twice already today," he said, his brow rippled in irritation. "But your papers are in order. Go through."

EPILOGUE
MARIA

Saturday, August 2, 1947, Toronto, Canada

My bedroom window was open, and a gentle breeze blew through the screen, making the light-blue curtains flutter in the shadows. But the air was too hot to provide relief from the muggy summer heat.

How I had managed to fall asleep for a few hours under the heavy feather comforter was a miracle in itself. It reminded me of that down comforter long ago when I was a child in Viteretz and I'd shared a bedroom with Krystia and Mama. Now I was halfway around the world with a room to myself on the second floor of Auntie Stefa and Uncle George's Franklin Avenue house.

Krystia and I had arrived in Toronto just two days earlier, and our aunt and uncle had tried everything they could to make our new home cozy and familiar. I had never had a bedroom of my own. The blue curtains reminded me of Mama's favorite blouse, and hanging on the wall was a copy of Mama and Tato's wedding picture. There was a framed photograph on top of the mirrored dressing table that represented my current family.

Auntie Stefa and Uncle George had driven all the way to Halifax to meet our ship when we arrived in Canada ten days ago, and as soon as our feet touched land, a photographer had snapped a picture of what he called our happy reunion. It wasn't actually a reunion, since we had never met before, but I did feel like I had known Auntie and Uncle forever. They had both written to me and Krystia at least once a week for the entire two years that we'd lived in the refugee camp, waiting to be approved as immigrants to Canada.

The drive from Halifax to Toronto was an astonishing experience in itself. Driving through this vast green country of lakes and ocean and rock, and of friendly people and houses and buildings that looked so new. Nothing had been bombed, and there were no piles of rubble or people waiting in line for soup. Each night we stayed in a different hotel and ate at restaurants, where Krystia and I ordered anything we wanted from sheets of paper with the choices listed on them. We had a chance to listen to Uncle George and Auntie Stefa tell us about themselves, their lives in Canada, and how excited they were to have us with them. By the time we got to this little house on Franklin Avenue, I felt like I had been a part of their lives forever.

I got up from my bed now and held the photograph closer to the window so moonlight shone on it at just the right angle. I touched Auntie Stefa's face—so much like Mama's. The jubilance of finally getting her nieces to Canada made her face radiant. Uncle George stood half a meter behind us three hugging, sobbing females, smiling with a quiet joy.

Just then, I heard a *thunk*.

I clutched the photograph to my chest. Which soldiers had come for us this time? Should I dive under the bed?

"Calm down, Maria," I whispered to myself. "You're safe. The war is over. You're in Canada."

But my heart still pounded. Would I ever be able to sleep an entire eight hours without a nightmare, or waking up sobbing? To not feel poised to bolt out of bed and flee at the first hint of danger? I had written to Auntie Stefa about my terrors at the refugee camp, and she said to give it time. Maybe now that I had a family and a home, a peaceful sleep would eventually come. But the thump was real, and I had to check it out.

I set the photograph back on the dressing table and wrapped my housecoat around my shoulders. I stepped out into the hallway and saw that Auntie and Uncle's bedroom door was closed. I opened it slightly to check on them. They were sleeping soundly, covers kicked to the floor; a hot breeze coursed through their room as uselessly as it did mine. I propped their door halfway open with the doorstop so they'd get a cross-breeze, then checked Krystia's bedroom.

It was empty.

My first thought was panic. That she'd been captured and taken away, but I forced that thought out of my mind. People get up in the middle of the night in Canada. Hadn't I just done that very thing? I tiptoed down the stairs as quietly as I could so as not to wake Auntie and Uncle.

Sure enough, there was Krystia, on her hands and knees on the kitchen floor, gathering up some scattered photos.

"What happened?" I whispered, bending down to help her.

"Minuit," she said.

That was Auntie Stefa's elderly cat.

"I was pouring myself a glass of milk and Minuit jumped onto the kitchen table and knocked down our photos."

"Pretty spry for her age," I said.

Krystia smiled. "I know."

I put some of the photos onto the table, and Krystia began to sort them out. I noticed the milk bottle still on the counter, so I got a second glass out of the cupboard and poured myself some too. I got a saucer and poured a bit for bad Minuit as well. After putting the bottle back in the refrigerator, I set Minuit's milk on the floor and mine on the table.

"You couldn't sleep?" I asked.

Krystia nodded. "It's so quiet, there's nothing to drown out my thoughts."

During the war, all thoughts were how to survive for the next minute. Rare bits of sleep were snatched while bombs went off overhead. In the refugee camp, we tossed and turned amid the belches, farts, groans, and tears of thousands. But now we were safe. No bombs, no one chasing us. We each had our own cozy bedroom and all the food, clothing, and love that we could possibly want. But the silence of the nights left plenty of time for memories and regrets. My heart ached, thinking about what our life might have been like if Hitler and Stalin had never been born. Mama would still be alive, and so would our friends and neighbors. Viteretz wouldn't have been destroyed. Ukraine wouldn't have been destroyed . . .

Almost as if she could read my mind, Krystia set her hand on top of mine and gave it a gentle squeeze. "Mama would be proud of us both," she said. "And so would Tato."

I knew if I tried to respond, I'd just start to cry, so I squeezed her hand and nodded. And I thought of our parents and their hopes and dreams for their daughters. I owed it to them to put the past behind and to live for the future. I'd try my best to do that, but it would take time. First, I'd have to learn to sleep an entire night with dreams of what might be instead of nightmares of the past.

I sipped my milk and sorted through the loose photos. Some were of Mama as a little girl with her brother, Ivan, and sister, Stefa. Some were from the refugee camp—of Mychailo and Birgit when they visited us from time to time. They had been accepted as residents of West Germany and had opened up a bakeshop together and were doing quite well. Whenever they visited, they would bring us some delectable treat like linzer cookies or strawberry pyrohy—without the sleeping pills, of course. There was a photo of Finn too, and one of his father. They would be arriving in Canada any day now. Elias's scheme had worked, and they'd been accepted as Dutch refugees. A distant relative in Kitchener had sponsored them. Once they were settled, we would visit them.

One of the photos was of Nathan, standing in front of the bridge in Zurich, Switzerland. He looked healthy, and so much older and more serious than the last time I had seen him in person. The last I'd heard, he'd found distant cousins and was moving to Israel.

"Are you excited about tomorrow?" Krystia asked.

Tomorrow. Something definitely to look forward to, and a happy thought to drown out the sadness.

St. Josaphat's Ukrainian Catholic Cathedral was not far from our house, and we'd be attending Divine Liturgy there for the first time. I looked forward to giving thanks for this new life that was opening up for me and my sister, and I also was looking forward to praying for the memory of all who had passed on before us.

The most exciting thing was what Auntie and Uncle had arranged for after the service. We were having an outdoor gathering with the local Ukrainian community.

"They all want to meet you," Uncle George had said. "They've heard so much about you."

"And there will be people your age," Auntie Stefa had added. "They speak English and Ukrainian, and some will be at the same high school as you in the fall. This will be the start of a new chapter in your lives."

"Not only that," Uncle George had said. "There will be cake."

I took another sip of milk and swallowed it, and then I leaned over and hugged my sister. "I am looking forward to it," I told her. "And I am so thankful that we can do this together."

AUTHOR'S NOTE

MY GREAT-AUNT WAS a sniper with the Ukrainian Underground during World War II, fighting both the Nazis and the Soviets. After the war, she was executed by the Soviets and buried in an unmarked mass grave. Her mother, my great-grandmother, was sent to a labor camp in Siberia. We can only assume that she died there, as we never heard of her again. Her name was Maria.

This book is a tribute to those who survived Hitler's frying pan but ended up in Stalin's fire.

Occupation Zones after World War II

Once the Nazis were defeated, the Allied nations (American, British, French, and Soviet) carved up what had been Nazi Germany into "occupation zones," taking the governance away from Nazi administrators and setting up new temporary administrations until order could be established.

Each occupation zone was flooded by refugees—sick and starving liberated concentration camp survivors and slave laborers, but also displaced Germans. Relief organizations worked with the military to provide food and first aid for the refugees. They also helped sort them out. Those who were German and deemed not Nazis were able to settle in the region. Those suspected of being Nazis were interned and processed through the criminal justice system.

Victims of the Nazis were sent back to their countries of origin when at all possible. This worked for victims from Western Europe because their homelands still existed, but for the majority, their countries had disappeared. Much of Eastern Europe, including what is now Poland and Ukraine, became part of the Soviet Union at the end of the war.

Repatriation

Joseph Stalin, the dictator of the Soviet Union, negotiated with US president Franklin D. Roosevelt and British prime minister Winston Churchill to have refugees who had lived in Eastern Europe before the war "repatriated" to the newly expanded Soviet Union.

To the British and Americans, this sounded like a

reasonable request. They also saw it as a practical solution to deal with the millions of homeless refugees from Eastern Europe who were living in temporary camps throughout postwar Europe.

What the British and Americans didn't initially realize was that Stalin considered any Eastern European who had survived Nazi occupation to be a traitor in need of punishment. The Soviet Union was an economy run on slave labor, and incarcerating refugees as traitors was an efficient way to get more slave labor. Stalin also did not want refugees to emigrate, because he knew that many were vocal critics of Soviet human rights abuses. Repatriating them was a way of silencing them. He was particularly interested in silencing resistance movements. Many of these had actively resisted the Nazis, and now that the Nazis were no longer a threat, had turned their resistance to the Soviets. Members of the Polish Home Army, the Ukrainian Insurgent Army, Russian anti-Soviets, and many German anti-Nazi groups were targeted.

Many survivors had no desire to be repatriated. Instead, they sought temporary asylum in the occupation zones administered by the British, French, and Americans. Their long-term goal was to be accepted into a country where all citizens had basic democratic rights.

When Stalin didn't get the flow of repatriates that he

expected, the Soviet secret police (NKVD) sent units into camps and forcibly removed people whom they claimed were their citizens. Some were sent directly into the Soviet Union as slave labor or shot outright, but those suspected of being members of a resistance group were placed into silence camps.

Once the other Allies realized that the Soviets were abusing refugees, they stopped allowing the Soviets to take them from their zones.

Internment Camps

Throughout the occupation zones in Germany and Eastern Europe, the Allies took over recently evacuated Nazi facilities and repurposed them into internment camps.

For the British, Americans, and French, these camps were used to process suspected Nazis. The Soviets also processed suspected Nazis, but their main focus was to identify people and groups whom they deemed as future threats to the Soviet way of life. They were particularly interested in identifying young people who could be future opposition leaders. Ironically, these were often members of anti-Nazi resistance groups, but the Soviets also targeted the pro-Nazi Werewolf group.

Instead of internment camps, the Soviets set up interrogation houses and silence camps.

A person suspected of working with a resistance group would be brought to an interrogation house, tortured into giving up names, and forced into signing a fictitious confession. The interrogation techniques and the holding-cell details in this novel are based on firsthand accounts. After the interrogation, if they were considered a low risk for agitation, they would be sentenced to slave labor. Those deemed agitators were either shot or jailed in a local silence camp.

The NKVD ran silence camps in East Germany from 1945 to 1950, but their existence was kept a secret from the West until after the collapse of the communist government of East Germany in 1990. They were called silence camps because people incarcerated there were allowed no contact with the outside, and even inside, the prisoners were isolated from one another. These camps were administered under the Soviet slave labor system (gulag) but were not labor camps. Inmates were not allowed to do anything. They received no medical treatment and little food. Many died of neglect. The silence camp that Krystia was about to be moved to in this novel was Special Camp No. 8 at

Fort Zinna. Ten thousand young people were imprisoned in silence camps.

Maria's daring rescue of Krystia was inspired by the prison break at the NKVD silence camp at Rembertów, near Warsaw, in which members of the Polish Home Army freed five hundred of their fellow fighters. In that instance, as in this novel, the guards were given sleeping pills ground up in their food. Escapes were rare from silence camps, so my characters escaped from an interrogation house, which would have been somewhat easier.

Border Move in July 1945

The Allied nations agreed beforehand which regions of Germany they would each be occupying once Germany surrendered, but the Americans purposely overshot their own region by about sixty miles, occupying regions of Thuringia and Saxony, which were supposed to be administered by the Soviets. The Americans did this in order to evacuate eighteen hundred German specialists and their families before they came under Soviet influence. They did not want the Soviets to have access to the specialists' information and expertise. The Americans withdrew on July 2, 1945, and the Soviets immediately occupied the area.

Occupation Zones, Germany

May 1945

SWED

DENMARK

SOVIET ZONE

NORTH SEA

JOINT AMERICAN-BRITISH CONTROL

GERMANY

Berlin ⊙

NETHERLANDS

Interrogation House

BRITISH ZONE

Torgau ⊙ ☆

SOVIET ZONE OCCUPIED BY AMERICANS UNTIL JULY 2, 1945

Dresden

BELGIUM

FRENCH ZONE

AMERICAN ZONE

LUXEMBOURG

American Refugee Camp

Karlsfeld ⊙

Munich ⊙

FRANCE

Lake Constance

N
W E
S

LIECHTENSTEIN

AUSTRIA

SWITZERLAND

0   50 MI
0   80 KM

ITALY

BALTIC SEA

SOVIET
ADMINISTRATION

EAST PRUSSIA

POLISH
ADMINISTRATION

SOVIET
UNION

Warsaw

POLAND

POLISH
ADMINISTRATION

CZECHOSLOVAKIA

Vienna

HUNGARY

ATLANTIC
OCEAN

EUROPE

Area of detail

YUGOSLAVIA

ACKNOWLEDGMENTS

I AM EXTREMELY grateful to the people at Scholastic Canada, Scholastic Inc., and Scholastic Book Fairs for enabling me to write my stories and to get them into the hands of readers. Dean Cooke, agent extraordinaire, thank you for your practical magic. Diane Kerner, thank you for your guidance and support over so many stories and books. Sarah Harvey, thank you for making the editing process so painless. Maral Maclagan, thank you for your expertise and persistence. Aimee Friedman, your encouragement and enthusiasm mean the world to me. Olivia Valcarce, thank you for your fine eye and your support. Yaffa Jaskoll, thank you for your stunning cover art and design.

Many thanks to Ludwik Klimkowski, board chair of Memorial to the Victims of Communism, Tribute to Liberty, who pointed me to first-person accounts of people incarcerated in special camps, particularly members of the Polish Home Army. I appreciate the vast number of personal memoirs written by survivors of Soviet interrogation and incarceration, as well as memoirs from Germans living inside the Soviet occupation zone immediately after the war. Details from those memoirs helped to bring this story to life. Anne Applebaum's beautifully written book *Gulag* was extremely helpful, as was Ulrich Merten's *The Gulag in East Germany: Soviet Special Camps, 1945–1950.* Thank you to my fellow authors, Karen Bass and Michelle Barker, for your conversations and research suggestions. And thank you for writing your own illuminating novels set in Germany after the war. Thank you to my sister Lara Forchuk and her colleague Lisa Wright. Their expertise in dog behavior helped me create a credible Roxy.

I am grateful to my father, Marshall Forchuk, for his recall of family history, including letters, tidbits, and conversations overheard about the fate of my great-grandmother and great-aunt. These small bits from the past have stayed in my heart for decades, making me yearn to find out more. A hug to Dorothy Forchuk, my dear late mom, for her unconditional love and steady confidence in my abilities, even in the face of my failing grade four. A kiss to Orest, my husband, whose patience knows no bounds and who is also a typo and fact-check sleuth. And a hug to my son, Neil, who takes after his father. This novel is very much about sisters, which is why it is dedicated to mine.

ABOUT THE AUTHOR

MARSHA FORCHUK SKRYPUCH is a Ukrainian Canadian author acclaimed for her nonfiction and historical fiction, including *Making Bombs for Hitler*, *The War Below*, *Stolen Girl*, *Don't Tell the Nazis*, and *Trapped in Hitler's Web*. She was awarded the Order of Princess Olha by the president of Ukraine for her writing. Marsha lives in Brantford, Ontario, and you can visit her online at calla.com.